THE
ARGENTINE
JOB

Movie Length Tales™ featuring:

Action and Adventure
Comedy
Drama
Horror
Kids and Family
Science Fiction and Fantasy
Thriller and Suspense

Ask for them in any bookstore, or see them all at:

www.AisleSeatBooks.com

JOB

A Movie Length
Action & Adventure Tale
For Readers
13 and up

Michael Penhallow

Lyme, New Hampshire

ISBN-13: 978-1-935655-60-2
ISBN-10: 1-935655-60-4
Library of Congress Control Number: 2012930941

Published by Aisle Seat Books, an imprint of
GrayBooks LLC
1 Main Street
Lyme, New Hampshire 03768

www.AisleSeatBooks.com

Softcover Edition

Printed in the Unites States of America on acid-free paper.

About Aisle Seat Books:

Read a good movie lately?

Every good movie starts with a script, and every good script tells a riveting story. Long before the actors are chosen and the filming starts, a writer sits down, crafts that story, and submits it for consideration by the producers, directors, and other creative talents in the film industry. It can take a long time. A script may spend years making the rounds before getting the elusive Hollywood "green light." If it ever does. Some of the greatest movies ever written are ones that none of us will ever see on the screen.

Aisle Seat Books finds the best of those not-yet-produced tales and brings them to you just as the writer envisaged them. Each of the books in this series has been converted by the script's author from the arcane shorthand of screenplay format into the familiar prose format you see here, a process called "novelization."

These little books are not novels, or even novellas. Think of them as written movies. Like the screenplays they come from, each is presented in real time, written in the present tense to allow you to "see" the movie's scenes in your mind's eye as if they were unfolding on a theater's screen before you.

So. Here's a movie. Take your favorite "aisle seat" and enjoy it.

Now Showing:

JOB

Action & Adventure
Ages 13 and up

Theater lights dim.

Fade in:

BUENOS AIRES, ARGENTINA

JANUARY 3, 0937 HOURS ARGENTINE
STANDARD TIME (ART)

It is hot, the type of heat where steam rises off the cobblestones and air-conditioning units work overtime. Taxis swerve in and out of the hordes of tourists. Not far away, legs, lots of legs, walk along the sidewalk and bodies swerve to the sensual music of the tango.

The scene is broken by a cartoñero, a street person who survives by collecting garbage and waste cardboard. The cartoñero wheels a heavy cart among the dancers.

He is followed by a three-legged dog who hops closely behind.

⇨

Tango dancers swirl before the horde of tourists who have disembarked from a newly arrived cruise ship. The tourists clap loosely to the beat. Slow motion, the classic dance of the tango: pulsing, sensual and romantic.

Watching in the crowd is a man dressed in a dark suit with open neck shirt and a briefcase at his side. He is dark, confident, and he could almost blend into the crowd if not for the thin scar that runs down the side of his face. Confidently, he walks through the crowd and approaches one of the newspaper kiosks which seem to adorn every corner of this city. He takes out 25 pesos and points to a prepaid Telefonica phone card.

0945 HOURS (ART)

A gentle wave breaks against the Mar del Plata beach. It is a typical January morning at the height of the southern hemisphere's summer; that period in the year when swarms of people come here to escape the exorbitant heat of Buenos Aires.

A pair of flip flops trounce along a train platform. Jeff Tully, early 30s, moves towards the arriving train. He is well toned, fit, a face scarred by experience but otherwise attractive.

"Permiso!"

The vacationers exit the train and run one by one. Eventually they disappear into the labyrinth of buildings that lead to the crowded beaches.

Isabella Pareña jumps out of a carriage and onto the platform. Twentyish, sexy, she strolls towards Jeff and instantly a smile breaks across his face.

He hands her a small bunch of begonias. She looks into his eyes and takes the flowers, smells them as she plants a kiss on his lips.

"Does this mean you've finally changed?" she asks.

She grabs his hand and they take off into the station and the mass of humanity.

2235 HOURS (ART)

Two hundred and fifty feet below the 20th floor, outside a tall apartment building, the Atlantic Ocean rhythmically beats against the Mar del Plata coast.

In the bedroom of one of the apartments Jeff slips his hand inside Isabella's blouse. Her breath quickens as he works his hands along her back.

LATER:

In the bedroom, the television flickers, a grainy image of CNN, breaking news. Isabella sits up in bed to listen to the anchor:

"Assassination in Buenos Aires, this time a diplomat and his family, killed in their home. The authorities have no leads. No surprises there."

She sits up and the light of the television flickers in her face.

Isabella turns to Jeff. "I'm scared, Jeff. The worst part is, I don't see it getting any better. Not after this."

"Come on," he answers. "Must you be so pessimistic?"

"You don't get it, do you?" she says.

He kisses her tenderly.

1635 HOURS (EST)

In a Homeland Security lecture hall in Washington, DC, Susan Taylor, smart and elegant, the new breed of Agency operative, stands at a lectern before a huge plasma screen.

Those in the front row stare at the image of a London Transport double decker bus in ruins.

"The Underground attacks in London, Madrid, or more recently in Moscow. Results that are far larger in instant headlines than in actual damage."

There are a few coughs, some fidgeting as Susan turns a page of her notes.

"This type of attack does not alarm us," she continues. "What does is the dirty bomb detonated in the middle of an urban center."

Susan notices the light blinking on her cell phone and reluctantly activates the Bluetooth earpiece while she continues:

"We begin with a rucksack or any old suitcase carried on board an international flight. Stand at a JFK arrival gate and you will see passengers flooding through with similar bags."

Susan listens to the phone.

"I'm sorry," she says to her audience. "You'll have to excuse me. My assistant will continue." Then, into the headset: "Yes?"

The assistant clicks and a short clip of a rucksack moving through the scanning machine appears on the screen. The assistant continues where Susan left off:

"Cobalt-60, used in radiotherapy. It is used for treating cancer. A US report last year recommended monitoring this material. Unlike a nuclear bomb, a dirty bomb does not involve nuclear fission and can be used like any conventional weapon."

"Argentina?" says Susan into her headset.

The assistant continues: "Tied to a C4 explosive, it would close the airport indefinitely and contaminate for several years."

"Tonight?" says Susan.

The assistant continues: "Think of the drama caused by the eruption of the Icelandic volcano. Well you can multiply that a hundredfold, maybe more."

2255 HOURS (ART)

Back in Argentina, in his apartment bedroom, Jeff's face nuzzles into the soft skin of Isabella's neck. Her eyes stare up at his, her look seems to say that she wants him. She smiles and starts to button up her blouse.

"A tango band," she says. "What do you think?"

He nuzzles his face into her back.

"I need to know the readings," she says. "You don't happen to have any favorites?"

Jeff stands up and reaches for his drink, a caipirinha, the Brazilian drink of choice. He gulps it down in one shot.

"No, I didn't think so," she says.

Jeff takes a deep breath. "Isa, I can't."

"What is this about?" she says. She sits up and leans on her elbow. Her face close to his.

"We have to talk," he says.

"How?" she demands. "I don't understand."

She looks away.

"Look at me, Isabella," he says. "I'm a loser, you're so much better than me.

JANUARY 4, 0927 HOURS (ART)

Inside a dilapidated department store on Calle Florida, the "Harrod's" sign shines into the bare room.

13

White sheets cover the remaining furniture but the store has been stripped bare, moth balled for a better, more prosperous time.

A large man enters the room and makes his way over to the bay window. He is dressed in full officer's uniform, a left over warhorse from the Cold War named Jason Ambrose. The U.S Military Attaché, a marine colonel named Ambrose, stretches his legs at the dining table and stares up at the old sign.

"You're kidding" he observes. "Harrod's, as in Knightsbridge, London. Down here?"

Susan looks a little tired yet still organized, always in control.

"Shut it down after the bank crisis," she answers. "Just waiting for the economy to recover. It'll probably open up again, despite London's objections!"

Next to her sits a man in his late fifties with a ponytail that sticks out of his side cap, brown hair that looks like it needs a good trim, wearing a standard blue suit, tie and patent leather shoes.

"Is it legal?" asks Ambrose.

The others look at each other and snicker. Susan answers him pertly:

The ponytail answers. "Sir, this is Argentina. It's all legal down here."

"Yes, right," answers Ambrose, a little embarrassed. "I wonder, Susan, can you fill us in on this nasty matter with the State Department?"

"Of course, sir." She checks her files. "State DSS conclude that the American ambassador was murdered."

"DSS?" says Ambrose. "I thought I knew all the acronyms."

"Diplomatic Security Service. Responsible for U.S. embassies around the world."

"Kind of a tall order recently," shrugs Ambrose.

A waiter arrives with some drinks and all discussions halt. Susan offers a cigar to Ambrose. He nods and she offers a light.

"You're telling me," says Ambrose, "Mr. Al Fayed hasn't closed the store down, patent infringement or something?"

"His lawyers tried," says the officer, "but gave up. Argentines have a healthy disrespect for international law."

The waiter exits and they return to the business at hand.

"So, Mr. DSS," says Ambrose to the ponytail. "What's your story?"

"Our main mission is to act as Americas eyes oversees."

"It was DSS who brought in Ramzi Yousef," adds Susan.

"The master of the original Twin Towers attack in '93," says Ambrose.

"America's best kept secret in the war on terror," answers Susan.

Ambrose offers his appreciation.

"This poor stiff in Buenos Aires," he then continues. "Do we have an explanation?"

"That's why we're here, sir," says Susan.

"So," asks Ambrose. "How does this story end?"

Susan looks at him. "Ambassador Macintosh was killed by an Al Qaeda assassin," she says.

Ambrose is genuinely shocked.

1005 HOURS (ART)

Jeff inhales the ocean air as he jogs along the deserted beach, his feet pounding out a steady rhythm against the sand. He is fit, takes good care of his body. He leaves the shoreline, heads inland towards a small restaurant perched up on the bluff.

1052 HOURS (ART)

It's early and the restaurant is dead. A stocky type, late thirties and wearing a Boca Juniors jersey perches on the bar. He sports plenty of tattoos and nurses a Quilmes beer. The maid avoids him and scrubs the floor around him.

The door opens and a delivery man enters with a sack of potatoes and frozen steaks. He dumps the load at the edge of the bar.

Jeff walks in. He picks up the pile of mail lying on the bar: bills, more bills and bank statements. He walks over to the register and opens it, taking out the small change and bank notes before locking back up.

"Que tal, Jeff?" says the beer drinker.

Jeff looks up. "Not bad, Rafael. You?" He straightens himself up.

"Bit of trouble at the estancia," says Rafael. "Usual gaucho crap—a lot of talk but no action."

Jeff grabs a pile of bills. With his foot he opens a file cabinet and places the bills on top of the already considerable pile.

"You'd let me know if you have anything?" says Jeff as he counts the money from the register.

"Really?" says Rafael. "I thought you'd be living extra large with your share of this place."

Jeff wraps the peso notes into an envelope and packs them in his briefcase. "It's not the money, it's Isabella. I can't go through that again."

Rafael takes another swig from his Quilmes as Jeff heads to the office. He takes a quick glance above the bar where a grainy photo of a younger Jeff and a beautiful woman hangs.

"You've got to move on," says Rafael. "Angie's gone. She's not coming back."

1104 HOURS (ART)

In the private back office Jeff thumbs through the receipts on his laptop. He checks that he is alone, closes the door quietly and sits down at his desk.

A few key strokes and he is on his personal account where his eyes are met by a steady stream of red arrows, all pointing down. He shakes his head.

From behind, he is startled.

"You're still a dreamer, Tully," says a male voice with an Armenian accent.

The voice belongs to a thick man in his late fifties. He wears an expensive suit, slicked back grey hair on top of a heavy set build. His presence rattles Jeff although he tries hard not to show it.

17

"How did you get in?" says Jeff.

"I own the place, remember?"

"Does that give you the right to come and go as you please?"

"No. The fact you owe me two million does. That's two million U.S. greenbacks, che, not this local peso crap!"

"You're going to have to give me more time, Gulassian," says Jeff.

"Sure," says Gulassian. "It takes time to make money. You know what bugs me, though? I don't see you working. Too busy with your local mujer."

Jeff stands and walks toward the window.

"We know where she dances, Jeff."

"She stays out of this."

"I say it takes her twenty minutes to walk home from the club, plenty of spots along the way where a couple of guys could pick her up."

"Fuck you!"

"A dancer, I'd say she uses her legs. My boys, you don't want to be on their wrong side. It might get ugly."

Jeff squares up to him, close enough to smell the stale cigar smoke on his breath.

"I'll kill you if you touch her."

"Just a hypothetical conversation."

He stares obliquely across the room, the photos of army buddies, all desert locations. "Just remember, down here you're one and we're many."

Jeff looks straight into his cold, dark eyes.

1127 HOURS (ART)

Back in Buenos Aires, a grizzled man with long grey beard walks toward the entrance of the King Fahd mosque. He is short and compact, looks decidedly older than his 53 years. His hair is greying but thick, his skin still smooth and velvety.

He bows as a pair of fellow Muslims arrive late for prayers. They scurry by, barely ten meters away.

He waits until they are gone. Then, and only then, he studies the man in front of him.

A young man, early 30's, wears a well tailored suit and on his face, a permanent grimace as if he's in constant pain.

"This way," says the older man in Arabic.

The side door slams shut behind them.

1135 HOURS (ART)

In the mosque's office the older man walks over to a large, golden desk and draws the curtains. The two men speak in Arabic.

"Do you have a cell?" asks the older one.

"Yes, Emir, I took care of it as soon as I arrived."

"Let me see."

The younger one empties his pocket and places the cell phone onto the desk. The Emir opens the cell, takes out the battery and checks the SIM card on his computer. "No good. The NSA might track this."

He replaces the SIM and plugs in the battery. "The brotherhood monitors all activity from here. From here on, Sallum, you have our protection."

19

He reaches beneath the desk, springs a latch and takes out a document, which he passes over to Sallum. "Everything has been planned with great care. The attack will strike terror and complete confusion."

Sallum reads intensely.

The Emir speaks in a calm, engaging voice as he unfurls an antique map. "The border lies open, all the way up to the Panama Canal."

He points to a spot in the north of Argentina. The border with Brazil and Paraguay.

"What the Americans are calling the Forbidden Zone," says Sallum.

The Emir nods slowly and folds up the map. "Cell phone activated, simple but effective."

"Very good," says Sallum.

"Any questions?"

"The others, the ones who brought me here. They have seen my face."

"No worries. They will return with their drugs for the Great Satan. I have informed customs. They will be caught at the border. They cannot betray you now."

Sallum speaks slightly under his breath: "I will taste sweet freedom and a sweeter death."

They clasp their hands together. Blood flows over their fingers into a silver chalice.

"The Prophet will stand at your side," says the Emir. "In sh'Allah."

1139 HOURS (ART)

Jeff stands at an office window that looks out at the expanse of the city.

The noise comes from down below. People bang drums, blow whistles and brandish slogans. Another demonstration in the streets.

The bank manager, a stiff, thickly mustached type, types some figures into his laptop.

He looks up apologetically from the screen. "I'm sorry, with no line of credit, there's nothing we can do."

He slams his laptop shut as if to make the point clearer as Jeff attempts to pull himself together.

"I could trade my way out."

"Mr. Tully, in this market, you'd be trading yourself further into debt."

"I made tons of money before. I could do it again."

The manager moves around the desk and looks out onto the tail of the demonstration, the dirty streets, slogans spray-painted onto the walls.

"Look, I don't usually do this but let me give you some free advice. The market is a tough game, do yourself a favor, stick to what you do best."

The manager walks to the door and holds it open.

1947 HOURS (ART)

The interior of Tully's flat is as low rent as his current life.

He slams the door and kicks his mail across the hall. Suddenly he sees a shadow from across the room. Movement.

He pulls out the Heckler Koch 9mm pistol tucked into the back of his waistband and crouches behind the counter ready for the sound of a silenced round.

21

Susan Taylor sits, cross-legged in the corner. "Why don't you come out from down there? You've kept me waiting long enough."

Jeff holds the handgun steadily in front. "Do I know you?"

She points to the gun. "Put it away. We need to talk."

She is dressed in a silk blouse and black dress, non threatening. Jeff sweeps the room, checks the curtains and looks back at her. He engages safety, holsters the 9mm automatic and approaches her.

"How did you get in?"

She ignores the question, stands up and moves away from the sofa. "Let's just say I'm here to help."

Jeff lets out a slight sigh of relief. "I could do with some of that."

"What's that?"

"Help. Haven't had much of that lately."

Susan checks him out once again. His baggy jeans taking the bulge of the HK, the slight suggestion of muscles under his t-shirt. "Actually, I know quite a lot about you."

Jeff stands close to her, looks directly into her eyes at the same time notices the thin line of pearls and the subtle scent of expensive perfume.

"Like I said, we should talk."

Jeff sits down next to her. 'Okay. I've got all day."

Susan gets up and walks towards the kitchen. She picks up an open bottle of wine, finds two glasses, blows the dust off the bottle. She checks the label and starts to pour. "Not bad, I like an Argentine Malbec. "

"Look, I'm not much for small talk, never have been. Do you have a name?"

Susan brings over the glasses. "Of course. How rude of me. Susan Taylor. Down here, I work for the Agency.

She offers her hand after passing him his glass.

"That much, I figured."

"And, I have a proposition."

Jeff takes a sip of the wine. A small grin forms on his face. Then it spreads across and he laughs to himself.

"What?"

"You're wasting your time."

"What makes you so sure?"

"I don't do that kind of work anymore. Don't they keep you informed about this stuff? Anyway, I don't risk my life, not anymore."

"Why's that?"

She takes a sip of the wine as Jeff looks at her tentatively.

"I'm trying to do what's right for me."

"Really? Making a right fucking mess of it, aren't you?"

"What do you know about it?"

He's starting to get annoyed.

"Like I said, I know you better than you know yourself. "

Jeff stands up, aggravated. "Fuck you."

He walks to the door but she persists. "Yesterday, you were visited by a man, Armenian mafia, collecting a debt. If you don't pay, you're dead. I can show you a few pictures of his work if you want, but you might need something a little stiffer than this. Last night you spent the night here, ordered a pizza and a few beers, this morning you met with your banker...want me to continue?"

Jeff turns around. He was just about to show her the door. "So, you are with the Agency."

Susan runs her hand through her hair. She stretches out her hand. "What do you have to lose?"

JANUARY 5, 1005 HOURS (ART)

The Faena Hotel is a hip, swanky hotel located in the Puerto Madero section of Buenos Aires. Housed in a red brick, former Victorian factory, its clients form a line at the check-in counter. Jeff hands the keys of his Ford Mustang GT to the doorman. He looks up, studies the outside of the hotel which towers above. It is early and he snakes his way through the über-chic, jet setting types that wouldn't seem out of place on the red carpet of the Oscars.

Susan joins him and leads him across the road, almost guiding him to the hotel entrance. "Nice wheels."

Jeff notices the wind catch her face, blowing a strand of hair across it. "Thanks."

Susan makes her way over the old cobbles and towards the entrance. "Too bad you fell behind on the payments."

She passes the doorman who opens the door for them. They enter into the stylish lobby, white silk muslin curtains hang from the rafters, a barman in the corner shaking up a house cocktail, the cool ambience a marked contrast to the blazing sun outside.

Jeff looks at her, puzzled. "I'm sorry?'

"You have until the end of the week before they take it."

Jeff shakes his head as she passes and heads along the hall. He falls in behind her.

He follows her over dark carpets, beneath crystal chandeliers and a French reproduction wooden armoire. She approaches the front desk.

"Room 1209. They're expecting us."

She doesn't need to look behind to know that Jeff following.

⇨

The interior of the junior suite is as impressive as the hotel lobby.

The double bed has been pulled away and a large ornate desk faces the windows that open up across the wide expanse of the Rio de la Plata.

A middle-aged man sits at the side of the desk. Behind him and peering over his shoulder stands a taller man in the olive green jacket of an Argentine officer. Jeff looks for somewhere to sit but nothing has been provided so he stands in front of the glass wall.

"So, you are Jeff Tully," says the man behind the desk. "Two years out of Delta Force, served eight years with distinction: Desert Storm, Bosnia, Afghanistan. Steady under fire, short-tempered, sometimes prone to violence?"

"I know my record," Jeff says bluntly.

The officer continues. "Not exactly officer material. Won't take advice from superiors or learn from mistakes. Would you say that's an accurate assessment?"

A cell phone rings. The officer mutters something in Spanish and then closes it.

The door opens and Susan enters. She perches herself on the oak desk, takes on a more professional, colder tone: "You understand that everything within these walls is confidential. You walk and you forget. Are we okay with that?"

Jeff nods briefly, indicating he has been through it all before with the Agency.

"Our target has tons of money, mostly hidden in the Middle East."

Again the officer perks up. "We gave them the squeeze, so they are looking for other havens—places to stash their cash."

"Yes, but I'm here in Buenos Aires. So why me?"

"We think it might be Latin America," says the officer pointing to a document before him.

"Do 'these people' have a name?" ask Jeff.

They all look at each other. Only Susan breaks the silence. "I suppose they do."

"Care to share it with me?"

"Al Qaeda."

There is an awkward silence which the officer breaks. "That's what makes us nervous, they are different, more organized and they've gone underground."

Jeff stares blankly out of the window.

2105 HOURS (ART)

The El Viejo Almacen is a Tango club that sits on a corner in the barrio of San Telmo, close to the government sector and the tourist hotels. The theater is barely half full since the cruise season is yet to begin.

Isabella dances on stage, oblivious to the catcalls that shout out from the front rows. The light sparkles off her garter, her high heels tip, she leans into her partner.

Jeff slugs from a beer bottle. It takes a few seconds for the reality to sink in and a moment to take out his cell phone.

He shows disappointment as he hears her voice.

"Susan?"

"You had no idea it would be Al Qaeda, right?

"How did you guess?"

"Look, we'll be behind you the whole way."

"Sure. I need some time to think it through."

"Understandable, but why the cold feet all of a sudden?"

"Simple. It's going to be dangerous and danger is the last thing on my mind right now." He closes the phone in time to hear the audience applause.

Isabella takes a long bow and exits the stage.

JANUARY 6, 1122 HOURS (ART)

The Faena Hotel looks good at any time of day, with the curtains drawn and the spotlights shining it takes on an intimacy that is hard to duplicate anywhere else.

The officer has taken off his army issued tunic as he pours out another coffee. "See, before 9/11, they kept their money hidden in offshore accounts. Luxemburg, Switzerland, the usual spots. But after 9/11 it all changed and the Feds clamped down."

The officer taps a few keys on the laptop and a projector displays a flow chart on the wall. "Like water, money has an amazing habit of flowing where it feels most comfortable. They call it hawala."

The projector shows a man in a UBS branch in Zurich, Switzerland.

"He's called Mohammed Emir."

The man exits the bank with a briefcase. He looks both ways and holds out his arm to hail a cab. He throws the briefcase into the rear seat and the cab speeds off.

The officer pushes pause on the projector. "Mohammed flies to Zurich, draws out say a quarter million Euros, goes to the nearest jeweler, buys gold, silver, diamonds..."

He pushes play and the video cuts to the interior of a jeweler's vault.

The Emir paws through huge quantities of gold, diamonds and other gems.

The officer stands and walks to the screen. "Sometimes he takes a plane to London or Paris. The CIA figures at least half a billion has been moved in the past month. You can see it in the commodity prices, gold at historic highs, shooting through the roof."

Jeff looks over at Susan. She doesn't say anything.

The officer pushes pause again. "As you probably already know, money kept in a bank can never be safe. The beauty of diamonds and gold is that you can liquidate at any time you choose, in any corner of the world. Cut it, set it, sell it."

"The fact is that the average American doesn't know he's supporting the bad guys by buying a ring for his sweetheart," the officer adds.

Susan walks up to the projector. "All the time al Qaeda keeps their money for when they need it. There's nothing the CIA, or anyone else can do about it."

She hits the power button on the projector and the room is dark for a few seconds before the lights come on.

1347 HOURS (ART)

Jeff puts the Mustang in gear and revs the engine a few times before taking off.

Outside of the parking lot, he pushes the accelerator and the Ford V8 growls as he heads north towards the city center.

Susan sits in the passenger seat, looking at the tourists arriving for the steak restaurants that abound on this side of the port.

"We want you to steal it, Jeff."

Jeff is silent for a moment. Then he looks at her. "Oh, that's all?"

Susan shrugs. "And you'd get to keep it," she says.

He pulls out onto the Avenida Mayo, past the Obelisk, slowed by the heavy traffic on Avenida Corrientes.

"Think it over, that's all we're asking," she says.

She sits in silence.

"How much are we talking about?"

Jeff accelerates along the highway.

"At least fifty million," she says.

Jeff is stunned for only a brief second but enough time for Susan to notice. He pulls the car over to the curb, cuts the ignition and turns to face her. "Jesus."

"Think about it, even after the fence, you're looking at thirty, at least."

"A five man team, six mil' each, I can do the math."

"Not bad for a few days work."

Her eyes catch hold of his, her expression lingers between sympathy and a direct challenge.

He tries to ignore her as he starts up the car and heads back into the heavy traffic.

2115 HOURS (ART)

The Las Brisas bar is empty at this time of the evening. A soccer game plays on the TV as Jeff and Rafael prop up the bar. Rafael O'Brien is one of those hardy mixes of Spanish/Irish decent.

"What do you know about her?" he asks.

Jeff takes a swig of his Quilmes beer. "Just that she broke into my flat and knows way too much about me."

Rafael helps himself to another. "The Agency look after their own, they never care about retired grunts like us."

"We'd be in charge this time," says Jeff.

"I could do with the work but I just don't trust them," Rafael replies.

"Rafa, we'd use our own team," Jeff says.

Jeff slaps him on the back and laughs nervously as he moves behind the bar and begins washing a pile of glasses.

Rafael passes his over. "Wouldn't have to fool around with this shit anymore, would you?"

They glance at the pile of unwashed dishes lying in the wash bins.

JANUARY 7, 1035 HOURS (ART)

Jeff is back in the same room at the Faena Hotel. This time he is offered a seat which he takes next to the same characters as the earlier meeting.

A bottle of mineral water sits on the desk, the window behind looks out onto the muddied, brown water of the vast Rio de la Plata.

The officer, dressed in the same olive green uniform, is the first to speak: "We know you must have several questions. The fact is there's been plenty of pirates attacking cruise ships recently. So this operation, if successful, wouldn't look out of the ordinary."

The officer continues: "According to our estimation, one man to steer the dinghy and four to assault the boat."

Jeff looks at Susan for a second. "That's all well and good but I'd like my own team."

"Actually we have our own people in mind."

31

There is an awkward silence before Jeff talks. "Like who?"

The officer turns towards the laptop. "The good American taxpayers went to a lot of trouble to turn you guys into killers. We keep tabs on everyone."

The officer takes a glance at Jeff. "Let's say men who need cash, badly."

He places a list of names on the desk.

Susan intervenes. "Jeff, it'll be a regular heist, so you'll need someone who works with explosives. And you'll need a fence."

"Don't worry, I've thought this all through."

"You can't just walk into Tiffany's with a bag full of conflict diamonds."

2115 HOURS (ART)

The interior of the El Viejo Almacen tango club is fuller than normal. The perfect place to talk business.

Jeff watches Isabella dance the tango with her dance partner. "I can't stand it, Sergio. I've been here almost three years now and never learnt the Argentine dance."

"It's their passion, not yours." Sergio is slouched, tall and dark with a rakish grin.

Jeff watches Isa take smooth, rehearsed steps around the dance floor. Her black silk dress flutters in the humid evening air.

Sergio takes a sip of the wine before him. "I'm out of that game, Jeff. I did my bit for Uncle Sam."

"If that's how you see it."

The male tango dancer tips his black fedora before he dips Isabella, her head dangles only a few inches from the stage as the crowd applauds.

Jeff looks up from his wine and shakes his head. "Well, I've got to be honest. I'm thinking about it."

Jeff can see the fear in Sergio's eyes. "Look, they want me to recruit. Men who need money, willing to take a chance," he says.

Sergio slams down his beer. "Assholes! I know they own my past but not my medical records?"

Jeff motions his hand. He doesn't want their conversation heard. Not here at least. "What's the problem? Are you dying on me?"

Sergio gets very serious and his eyes glaze over. "No, worse than that. It's my kid. He has a hole in his heart...only known cure is stateside. Southern California."

Jeff is really moved by this. "Christ, I'm sorry."

Sergio takes another swig. "What choice do I have? Down here he doesn't stand a chance, he'll die."

"What are you going to do?" Jeff asks

"The doctors say it's one chance in a hundred. You don't know what it's like. Think of the worst times and multiply by ten."

"Could you fly him back?"

Sergio slaps him on the back. "If I had half a mil' laying around, but, hell, I don't even have insurance on my car. I came down here to disappear. The problem is I didn't know my money would, too."

Jeff turns to go but Sergio grabs his arm, gives him that telling look.

33

"It's deniable, only token help from the Agency."

Sergio's eyes have turned a reddened hue. "How much?"

"More money than any of us could spend in a lifetime."

Sergio laughs bitterly. "I'll believe that when I see it."

"No, this one's for real. What's the big deal anyway?" Jeff rests his hand on Sergio's shoulder. "It's just panning some rocks from a bunch of really bad dudes."

Sergio takes a long look at the bill but Jeff puts a 100 pesos note down.

"I promise, that's all."

2302 HOURS (ART)

Jeff pushes the fob button and the Mustang's lights blink. He stops to admire the vehicle for a second.

He turns and goes inside his apartment building, then heads to the elevator in the apartment hall.

On the seventh floor, he takes his keys out of his pocket, hears a slight movement behind him, and looks back; nothing. So he ignores it. Suddenly he is pushed into the wall, arms held at his side. Then all he hears is heavy breathing as he cannot move his head.

Ricardo Gulassian is a heavy man. His tight suit does nothing to hide the large gut that sticks out over his silver buckled pants. "I've had enough of your games. You know what I want."

"That's all well and good. There's just one problem."

"Yes?"

34

"I don't have it."

Gulassian holds a gun to Jeff's temple. "Too bad."

Gulassian pushes him inside the apartment and turns on the light. The lamp illuminates Susan, who also holds a gun.

Susan is the first to speak. "I'm offering you a job. Are you up for it?"

Gulassian laughs out loud. "Listen to her, Jeff. I don't see any other choice."

Jeff looks into Susan's eyes. "Okay, okay. I'll do it."

He looks over at Gulassian who wears a masochistic grin on his face.

Susan turns around. "And why should I believe you?"

"Because it's either you, or it's him," Jeff answers.

She looks over at Jeff and then turns to see Gulassian who has lit a cigar and blows the smoke calmly above his head.

Susan pulls the gun up and in one swift motion fires a double tap into Gulassian's head. He slumps over and falls instantly to the floor.

Jeff is completely stunned. "What the fuck?"

"Like I said, you scratch my back."

2352 HOURS (ART)

The sun shines through a shallow crack in the curtains of Jeff's apartment. It forms a thin slit that shines across a rolled up Persian rug that now contains the dead body.

Susan slings her jacket over the sofa. The rest of the apartment is well furnished, polished oak floors lead to a full kitchen. Jeff pours into a silver shaker and prepares the drinks.

"You seem annoyed by the proposition," she says as she sits down.

"If that is what the Agency gets up to down here."

"Look, Jeff. You needed a little persuasion, that's all. Take this job and you'll be out of here in a few weeks. No one will know or care. Now, I'm a little thirsty, what do you have?"

He pours out some lime juice and liquor, shakes up two caipirinhas.

"Do you have an idea for the team?"

He nods his head. "They don't know the facts, so maybe they'll back out. But they all need money, and fast."

She smiles and he sees the sparkle in her eyes. "Good. I knew you could do it. That's why I chose you."

"There'll be one other guy. His family runs the docks in El Tigre."

Susan nods her head, knowingly. "Your future brother in law?"

"Don't tell me you know about him?"

Susan taps her temple. "Remember who I work for." She throws back her hair. "Look, he's gay, not exactly discrete about it. Doesn't stop him from being a tough guy but he's not exactly cutting it, is he? I hope you haven't told him the plan."

"Everyone needs a motive," he says.

"Could be a little risky."

"Susan, it's not that easy. I need someone I can trust. He knows the waters and most importantly when the time comes, he'll fence the goods."

"You don't need to be so suspicious of us, Jeff."

Jeff thinks for a second. "But I am. You see, we've all learned the hard way. If we don't have control there's no deal."

Susan swills her finger around the rim of her glass and drinks it down. "Okay, no objections. As long as Al Qaeda doesn't have their money, that's all we care about."

She unwraps a leather pouch of crisp Argentine banknotes and places it on the kitchen counter.

"That covers that angle."

"What is it you put in those drinks?"

"It's Brazilian. Derived from sugar cane."

Clearly amused, Susan saunters over to him. She kisses him softly on the lips and pushes him back onto the sofa. "That's not what I'm talking about."

For a moment he yields but something about this doesn't feel right and he pulls back.

"Something wrong?" she asks

"No, nothing."

Slowly she smiles and then catches a glimpse of a framed photo of Isabella. "Is she going to replace your wife?"

"I said I'd never speak about that."

He doesn't want to admit it, but cannot help it. "No," he says.

Susan continues. "Anyway, I thought it was over with her."

"I promised I'd never do this work again. I'm only going to break one vow tonight."

Susan circles around him. "Oh sure, the big dilemma; one more job and it's all over."

"Is there anything wrong with that?"

"It's bad luck. Plus I've heard it all before."

Susan senses that his mood is changing. "By the way, I looked through your file."

"Anything interesting?"

She runs her hand through his hair. "Nothing worries you, does it?"

"Apart from the fact I have a dead Armenian gangster to ditch and I'm about to steal fifty million from Al Qaeda."

She gets up to leave and brushes her hand gently across his face. "I like that in a man."

She pulls him into her and closes the door behind them.

JANUARY 8, 0932 HOURS (ART)

The pale sunlight shimmers on the double paned, bulletproofed windows. Crowds below chant slogans against the IMF, or is it the World Trade Organization, the international banks or the Peso devaluation? It is hard to tell up here in the air conditioned palatial splendor of former President Juan and Evita Peron's personal quarters.

The interior of the Casa Rosada is cooler than usual. But not from the overworked air conditioning that operates throughout the building, more from the two characters that stare at each other across a baroque, gilded antique desk.

The other man offers a Cuban cigar to the U.S. Military Attaché, Colonel Ambrose.

"Do you have an answer for me, Mister President?" asks Ambrose.

The President exhales and the smoke drifts briefly over the marble sculpture of his idol, Juan Peron, and up into the cut crystal chandelier that hangs precipitously above.

"Your own newspapers suggest Al Qaeda operates within this country," continues Ambrose. "Yet you seriously profess to know nothing about it?"

The President thinks deeply for a moment as he plays with a globe that sits on the side of his bureau. "How can I know everything? If they are here, as you say, why don't you catch them?"

"Because we need your help."

"This is a large country. We have many problems."

He looks out to the masses below. The President turns around to face Ambrose.

"I have a question for you. Your former president, on that fateful day in 2001, did he know that terrorists were training on U.S. soil? Did he know when they would strike?"

1804 HOURS (ART)

Jeff crosses the Avenida Dorrego, followed by two of his new team, Tulio Pareña, tall and lanky, and Rafael as they enter the Mercado de Pulgas, Buenos

Aires's main flea market. The two team members stick close to Jeff as they head deeper into the warren of vendors, where the roof hides the shady deals taking place.

The small rooms are stacked full to the ceiling with junk, furniture, spectacularly bad paintings, bedsprings and car parts.

Jeff enters into a small office and closes the door behind him. Only a single bulb illuminates the interior and he makes out a big man who stubs out his cigarette and stands. Late forties, heavyset but well dressed, he tries to size Jeff up. "Were you followed?"

Jeff sits down at a desk. "I took procedures."

"You can never be too careful around here."

Jeff lifts up his leg and unzips a pouch. He pushes it over the table. "To show we are serious."

The big man checks the crisp pesos, runs the freshly printed money through his hands. He grabs his jacket from the back of the door, stuffs the wad of money in his pocket and opens the door.

1915 HOURS (ART)

The sun begins to set across the Rio de la Plata. On one side of the dock Jeff prowls along the edge of the jetty, his face illuminated by the stub of a hand rolled cigarette hanging from the corner of his mouth. He approaches a dock worker.

"Do you know the way to La Boca?"

The dock worker stares at Jeff as he spits out the cigarette, stamps it into the cobblestone jetty. "Too far to walk, we'll have to take a cab."

Jeff checks him up and down; no subtle bulges at his side, no glint of back up. He waves Tulio over, who emerges behind them driving a car in the telltale colors of a Buenos Aires taxi.

The two of them enter the taxi and Tulio drives off. He checks the rear view mirror for any tails and heads back to the port.

The Taxi drives between cars, rusted metal, train tracks, shipping containers. Eventually they come to an old warehouse and he swerves to a halt. Jeff pays and they exit.

Outside the air is still and warm for the evening. A few kids play soccer on the sidewalk, otherwise there are no signs of life.

Jeff follows the dock worker to a dimly lit pier which opens up onto the murky brown waters of the polluted river.

A tug boat is tied up to the jetty.

Jeff walks up to the El Madryn. It is a rusty freighter, about 90 feet long, a black metal hull, two rusty cargo cranes bolted onto the deck.

The dock worker waves for them to follow. "Vamos."

Jeff looks around and walks up the gangplank. He is followed by Tulio.

Jeff notices that the bridge is equipped with radar and a modern GPS locator. A brand new black inflatable Zodiac is strapped to side of the boat, next to a long grappling hook.

"Where's the crates?"

The dock worker leads them across to the hold. He reaches around and clicks a switch on a single battery powered electrical light, enough to illuminate the four crates stacked against the wall.

Tulio takes a look at the stranger as he walks closer. "We'll need a moment, please."

The dock worker looks at his watch, turns and leaves reluctantly.

Jeff takes out his crowbar and opens the first crate: two Makharov sniper rifles, two Heckler & Koch automatics, ten magazines for each gun, holding 30 cartridges each.

"What if we hit real trouble?"

Tulio checks his crates. Inside each are 3 two-pound blocks of Semtex which he slits open with a knife. He sniffs it, plays it in his hands. It looks like modeling clay as he plays with it as a child does with play dough.

"This is good stuff," he says.

1945 HOURS (ART)

Back at the El Tigre docks, the taxi brakes hard at the train tracks and parks by the side of the El Madryn.

The team peels out to begin unpacking the gear. Crates are loaded one by one onto the gangplank and up into the ship.

Inside the freighter, the crew are actively laying the kit out for inspection. The low hum of the engines fills the small cabin.

The contents of the crates lie all around, guns hang over the bunk beds. Each member of the team is busy standing over the equipment and checking each item. Except Sergio, who sits and reads a thick book.

"What is that you're reading?" asks Jeff.

Sergio closes the book and looks up. "Nothing."

"Looks like something to me," Jeff says.

Sergio puts the book in his bag. "It's about the Crusades."

Jeff checks the extra magazine and tapes it to the side of a Makharov sniper rifle. "A little light reading?"

"History, that's all."

"Yes, what about?"

"This stuff. It's has been going on for thousands of years, that's all."

Jeff checks the springs and reloads the copperhead rounds. "What stuff would that be?"

"Oh, you know. Terrorism."

"What?"

"It's just a modern day hashishin."

"Say what?"

"Hashishin...assassins. The word comes from a hashish pipe, do you know that?"

"You smoking that stuff now?"

Sergio ignores him. "It's derived from the ancient Arabian concept of hashishin; a captive group of assassins kept faithful by a constant supply of the drug."

Jeff looks skeptical.

"Don't worry. I don't smoke...at least not before a job."

43

2358 HOURS (ART)

At the El Tigre docks the exterior of the freighter is highlighted against the dockside cranes.

The men are busy loading weapons, magazines carefully taped to the sides of rifles. Supplies are ample, they have enough firepower to start a small war.

Rafael looks over at Tulio. "Say what you want about the Agency, it's good to have them on our side."

Tulio looks up in dismay. "What? Have you forgotten how they treated us?"

"Sure, but they've planned for this one."

Tulio whistles through his teeth and shakes his head. "I don't agree."

Jeff enters and the bickering stops. "Right, listen up," he says.

The team stops their packing and each take their seats.

Jeff continues. "As we know, the target is a converted luxury yacht. You've seen the rusted hulks all over the Rio de la Plata, so it should stand out like a sore thumb."

JANUARY 9, 0135 HOURS (ART)

The freighter sails alone on the vast expanse of the Rio Plata. It is merely a tributary of the Tigre Delta, but from here it may as well be in the middle of the Atlantic Ocean.

The team stand on the bridge, eyes affixed to the radar.

Jeff is still going through the last checks. "C4?"

Tulio moves forward. "Check."

"Zodiac tied up and ready?"

"Check. Filled with gas and one extra jerry can."

Jeff approaches the pilot and puts his hand on his shoulder. "This is as far as she takes us, Fernando. We'll need you to look after the dinghy from here on. Entiendo?"

Fernando seems ready for action. "Si, senor."

0157 HOURS (ART)

Fernando stands on the stern as the salt water sprays against his face. He steers the rubber dinghy towards the rising moon.

Jeff checks the Makharov sniper rifle; bullet in the chamber, safety engaged, extra ammunition strapped to his belt.

Rafael is itching for action. "Okay, enough talk. We've gone through this enough times, let's get on with it."

Jeff ignores Rafael, holds up the GPS device and takes a reading. "Fernando, when we board the ship you keep it close. Got it?"

"Claro."

"Keep us in sight at all times. Don't want to get lost out here."

"Si, senor."

Jeff turns off the lit screen. "Three clicks right."

On the radar screen blinks the green dot of the target straight ahead. Moving at a steady pace of 8 knots, the dinghy is rapidly gaining on the target.

Jeff is focused on the target. "Alright guys. Goggles on."

The salt water spray hits his face as Fernando revs the engine. Jeff gathers the team around as Rafael is about to lose his lunch. Again.

Jeff kneels down in the center. "An old master sergeant drummed it into me. See the enemy before he sees you."

He holds up the GPS. The target still appears as a tiny green blip on the screen.

Jeff continues. "One degree right. Got it?"

Tulio is on his right. "Clear as daylight, target acquired."

0204 HOURS (ART)

The dinghy begins to rock back and forth as it approaches the wake. Rafael throws up again, Jeff looks down to the puke mixing with the seawater running down the side of his wet suit.

He looks up to concentrate on the job at hand.

0235 HOURS (ART)

The Al Hadiga is a 250-foot luxury yacht converted into a high tech trawler, except its payload is not black gold but the real thing itself. The twin engine Detroit Alison 8,000 horsepower motors purr at low revs. The pilot spots the Montevideo ferry and steers a route that takes him further out to sea, away from the Uruguayan coastline.

Behind the bridge the early morning is calm. A game of backgammon, some Arabic music in the background and prayer mats scattered on the floor for the evening prayers. All that illuminates the scene is the thin gloomy haze of the radar.

Suddenly the radar pings and a head turns towards the monitor.

0243 HOURS (ART)

Outside on the River Plate estuary, the team have by now accustomed their eyes to the darkness.

The growl of the target ship drowns out the sound of the dinghy's engine. Jeff pulls down his night goggles and switches them on. The target sits before him. A white luxury yacht posing as a cargo ship.

"Not exactly a typical vessel in the South Atlantic."

Jeff passes the glasses over to Tulio. "All that money pouring into the Brazilian economy has to go somewhere, I suppose."

"Right. A new toy for a newly minted Brazilian billionaire."

Jeff sees no movement on deck. Through the goggles, he can see the heat from the engine, but that is it.

Jeff turns back to the team. "This might be easier than we expected."

He turns round as the engine noise audibly lowers. Tulio lowers the revs as the dinghy heads for the calmer water of the ship's wake.

Jeff looks carefully through his rifle scope.

"Contact! Second mast, one click to the left."

Jeff moves the sniper rifle and levels onto the target.

He zooms into the target. Beyond the stacks of cargo containers, he spots a green flare, someone smoking on the deck.

Tulio reads the radar. "One fifty and closing."

Tulio pulls on the throttle. "Throttle down."

Jeff looks up to the ship as the green blob paces back and forth nervously. He holds the rifle tightly to his body, breaths steady, struggling to find the perfect balance as the boat rolls through the wake. The crosshair flows across the ship and onto the green blob. He raises it up a few inches above the forehead and holds steady sucking his breath deep inside.

Jeff squeezes the trigger and the rifle kicks back against his shoulder as the bullet flashes through the night sky.

Rafael checks the deck through his night vision goggles. The green blob lies on the deck motionless. "That one's for Allah."

He kisses the gold cross around his neck.

"Enough with that crap!" Tulio sparks up.

"Why?" Rafael asks tauntingly

"Because it's bad luck."

They are closer to the ship now. The spray pours down, covers their faces with saltwater. Silently, they drift towards the ship.

The huge engines begin to draw them towards the props, the tips of icy steel visible through the churning water.

Jeff reloads the rifle and places it back on his shoulder. "Careful now. Put it into reverse."

The outboard engine whines above the slow hum of the turbine. They are pulled back from the props and move closer to the stern. Rafael stands up and hurls a grappling hook onto the deck. Metal clanks on metal, but it falls back into the brown, muddy water.

"Fuck it," Jeff whispers under his breath.

Rafael throws it again, this time it falls between two pallets. He pulls it hard and the pallets slide against a railing until the rope snaps tight.

Rafael holds the line steady. "I'll cover."

Jeff is the first over the top and hauls himself onto the rope ladder. Three rungs up a wave slaps against his body. He loses balance and for a moment he is sucked down towards the propeller. Right hand still on the rope, he heaves once more with all his might, salt water stinging his eyes. For a brief second he sees the prop's metal shaft shimmer in the muddy water and then dive back down into the brown depths of the wake.

One last heave and he steadies himself on the deck. He holds the rifle to his eye, surveys the deck: 80 feet of bare metal, two cranes to the side and a lifeboat. Lying by the lifeboat a crumpled, lifeless body with a cigarette still smoldering at the side.

Jeff leans back and gives a thumbs up. The rest of the team silently begin heading up the rope ladder.

Ahead, Jeff can see the bridge, a dim light protruding from above. Only the metallic sound of radio music is carried by the wind.

Three sharp shots ping off the steel deck.

Jeff shouts into his headpiece, his voice hidden beneath the roar of the engines: "Contact!"

He looks behind in time to see Fernando take two shots in his abdomen and fall back into the dinghy.

All four men lie flat on the black metal, blackened up, out of sight. Tulio grabs the rope and ties it to the ship. He yelps as the rope eats into his wet hands. He looks behind him as more shots ring out. Tulio goes back to the dinghy. He finds Fernando on the floor of the dinghy, checks for a pulse.

"Situation report?" Jeff asks.

Tulio checks beneath his neck. "Negative, he's gone."

Tulio climbs back aboard the freighter.

Jeff whispers into his mike: "Shit, there's more. Two up."

Jeff covers the stairs as Rafael and Tulio enter the shadows and climb on to the bridge. Rafael waves two fingers; targets acquired. Jeff nods again and this time Rafael moves up.

There are four silenced shots in quick succession and then the metallic clank of a door banging on the deck. He watches as shots echo along the ship. Through his scope he sees a man on the wheel spin round as a hydrostatic shock rips through his body. A second man reels on his feet and staggers away, holding his shoulder. Injured but alive.

Rafael sparks up on the intercom: "He's wounded."

A few seconds of silence as Rafael pursues the target, Jeff sweeps the bridge for more threats. Then he hears a hail of bullets, this time followed by movement, running to the hold. For a split second he sees a dark bearded man, blood streaming down the side of his face.

He is heading for Rafael. Jeff holds the rifle steady.

"Hajaba! Hajaba," the bearded man shouts in Arabic.

He has a gun and points it towards Rafael. More shots, as Jeff covers the deck and Rafael dodges a shot which pings off the hull. Rafael shoots off a few rounds until his gun jams.

"Stoppage!" Rafael yells above the din.

Jeff puts in a few covering rounds until a thud splinters behind. He falls back onto the deck.

The Arab steadies his aim but blood pours down his face obscuring his vision. He wipes off the blood.

Jeff levels his scope and holds his breath.

The shot is true and the bullet explodes between the man's eyes, sending the body backwards, his mouth wide open. Jeff runs up to Rafael, covers the open hatch.

"You okay?" Jeff asks.

"Bastard got me in the arm," Rafael's voice is shaking, the adrenaline rushing through his veins.

Jeff tears the shirt away to reveal a wad of flesh and blood.

"Don't worry, I'll be okay. But there are more down there, I can hear their voices."

Jeff is already in paramedic mode. "Give me your kit. I'll try to stop the bleeding."

Jeff rips open the package and shoves a gauze into the wound. He applies the gauze and tapes it up.

Behind him he hears two more shots. Tulio scurries toward the thick steel door and heads for the hold.

0342 HOURS (ART)

The ship cruises on autopilot through the dirty brown waters of the Rio de la Plata estuary. They are still 20 nautical miles from land but the lights of the city are beginning to show on the horizon.

Jeff has made his way to the thick door and the entrance to the hold. He peeks around the corner, checking for any bodies. Nothing, so he enters the hold. It is complete darkness. Jeff chucks in a flare and the room is ignited by a cold, steely aurora. Tulio climbs down behind him.

Jeff is the first to break the silence. "This is going nowhere fast. We'll have to force them out."

"That's what I wanted to hear," a smile forming on Tulio's face.

"Yeah, right. Just don't go sending us to the bottom."

A few more steps down the stairs before a short burst of gunfire shatters the silence and they move further up the stairs to relative safety.

Tulio has his bag set before him. "Give me a couple of minutes."

He opens up the small case and takes out a brick of grey plastic. He breaks off a blob and forms a small ball in his bare hands. In this he sticks a tiny detonator and two prongs onto the glob. Jeff presses his ear against the thick steel door.

Rafael has finished his checks. There is nobody left on deck. He looks out at the distant lights. "That's the city on the horizon."

"Enough with the sightseeing," says Jeff. "We need to finish this, now!"

Tulio holds a black taped package wired to a 9 volt battery. He forms the contact, a light bulb glows.

Tulio looks up at them. "I know. This stuff scares the hell out of me too."

The other two exchange glances.

Tulio joins the two wires with a Chinese pigtail. He tosses the plastic bomb down the full length of the stairway and they all run behind the deck and cover their heads.

They don't have to wait long for the explosion. It rips through the ship's structure as smoke fills every crevice of the room.

After the dust settles, Jeff moves up first, his rifle held out before him, ready to shoot at anything that moves.

He moves towards a shape, clears the debris and sees the head is severed from the body. A man in two parts, blown in two.

He looks up at the bunks, rows of postcards, burnt Korans open at specific pages. The walls are lined with photos of relatives, girlfriends, some of them still smoldering at the sides.

Tulio peers around the door jam. "Five beds, only three bodies. There's got to be more down here."

Jeff moves on down the corridor. He stops at a small ante room, sweeps the room with his gun and comes upon two bolted steel doors.

He pulls off his rucksack and lays it on the table. Tulio is behind him and moves forward to inspect the huge, steel door.

Jeff gets on his knees, tries to see anything beneath the door. But there is nothing, not even a crack of light. "They're in there with the gold and diamonds," he says.

Tulio takes out a tape measure and measures the sides.

"Fuck it, this is close to ten inches thick. That wasn't part of the plan!"

"I don't give a shit about the plan. Can we get in?" Jeff asks.

Tulio runs his hand over the locking mechanism, massaging the safe. He moves over the hinges, the joint where the door closes.

Tulio looks up to him with a frown on his face. "I'm not sure."

"What the fuck does that mean?"

"Just that. But, and it's a big but, every safe has its Achilles heel."

Tulio is still running his hands over the door.

"So where is it?" Jeff asks.

"I don't have the foggiest."

"Great. What's the chance of blowing a hole in the hull?" Jeff asks.

"I'm not a gambling man."

Jeff gives him a look. He needs more, one last effort.

Tulio begins to think aloud. "Position the plastic, the force travels on a horizontal axis. Shoot directly into the crack will blow a hole about a fist size, can't stop part of the energy going up, or down."

"What are you talking about?" Jeff asks.

"Just that without a deflector, I can't direct the blast. It could blow us to the bottom of the sea."

"Great, that's reassuring," Jeff replies.

Rafael has so far been a silent observer. "I say we take a vote."

"Nothing to eat or drink. They're going to come out at some stage, whether we shoot them or not," Jeff says.

But Rafael won't budge. "We're close to the city. They might call for help. Maybe a radio, a satellite phone or something."

Tulio has his bag of tricks at the ready. "They are fanatics. They might just decide to die in there instead of handing over Allah's gold."

Rafael nods his head in agreement. "I say we blow the bastards."

"Me too," adds Tulio.

"That's it, then," says Jeff.

Tulio has already worked two balls of C4 into packets of plastic that he carefully squeezes into the long, thin cracks.

Jeff checks his watch again. "Come on, Tulio, we don't have forever."

He motions for the others to move back and gives the sign to Tulio.

55

All but Tulio exit onto the deck and hide behind a stack of well used pallets. It is silent and pitch black apart from the dim lights of the city as Tulio clambers onto the deck and dives for cover.

The blast shakes the ship several feet above the waterline, seawater splashes over the side onto everyone and down into the hold.

From below they can hear the sickening sound of creaking metal, joints breaking out of position.

Jeff moves forward into the smoldering mess. The cabin is hard to make out through the smoke, nothing more than a mess of twisted metal scraps litter the floor. Jeff's eyes lock on a figure of a man, sprawled across the floor. Legs severed clean from his body, blood still pumping from the abdomen

Suddenly a voice shouts out from the smoke: "Rahmet! Rahmet!"

Jeff whispers under his breath, "Sorry, pal, not today."

He fires two shots into the man's forehead. By now Tulio and Rafael are beside him, holding their guns out, covering all angles.

Jeff moves further into the room. One other man lies motionless, dead in the corner. Then another, a gaping hole opened in his chest where a chunk of steel door has cut straight through.

Then they hear the faint sound of running water.

Tulio moves forward straining to hear. "Shit, that doesn't sound good."

"Is that water?" Jeff asks.

Tulio heads down the stair well, shines the torch. "Afraid so. It's coming in pretty fast."

Rafael is now with them. He looks over at Tulio, hatred in his eyes. "Stupid Gaucho faggot! I knew we couldn't trust you!"

Jeff stands between them. "Enough! We've still time to get this stuff off before she goes down."

Rafael stares through Tulio, moves his aggression onto the neat stack of small wooden crates. The heavy boxes are stacked on top of each other.

Jeff grabs the first box and hands it to Rafael who stands on the top rung. Tulio heaves the boxes up to the dinghy. Box after box move up to the top as the water swirls higher and higher around their knees.

The water is rising fast, it is almost up to Jeff's waist. He holds up his hand. "We should go, there's only a few left."

But Rafael won't hear of it. "We've come this far. We take it all."

"Don't be a fool. There's no point if it all goes to the bottom!" This time it is Tulio.

Rafael jumps up and stabs his finger into Tulio's chest. "You got us into this mess!" says Rafael.

Again Jeff stands between them.

"Will you two shut the fuck up! As long as it doesn't go to Al Qaeda, what does it matter?"

He passes up the last two boxes.

Jeff points to the ladder. "The sooner we're out of here, the better. Any sign of our ship up there?"

Tulio drags the limp body of one of the dead and tosses it down into the hold. Rafael, calm now, scans the horizon for signs of the ship. Nothing.

Jeff scans the empty horizon. "He's got to be out there."

They stack each box onto the Zodiac dinghy, belting them into place so that nothing can fall over the side. Meanwhile, the water has begun to wash over the deck of the doomed freighter.

Jeff grabs his radio and tries a contact: "Bravo 235, come in?"

There is a garbled crackle but nothing else.

"What the hell is keeping him?" asks Rafael.

A wave rolls over the ship, eerie creaks of the structure drown their voices as the last of the boxes is hauled onto the dinghy and tied into place.

But now there is no room left for any of them.

Jeff looks at the men. "We're going to have to swim for it."

Rafael gives Tulio an angry glance, pulls on the life vest and jumps into the water. Tulio follows, holds onto the side as Jeff takes one last look at the doomed yacht.

Jeff enters the water behind them. "Let's push the dinghy away from this thing before it sucks us under."

They struggle to keep their heads above water, moving the dinghy away from the sinking ship. Jeff reaches for a side compartment, unzips the interior and pulls out a flare gun . He points it up and shoots it far above them.

The flare shines harshly beneath the mist and he can see the tired look in their eyes and the last gulps of the dying ship as it sinks beneath the turbulent sea.

The swell subsides and they float silently in the wake. From afar a light shines on them, illuminates the three of them as they hang onto the dinghy and its precious cargo.

A small light, floating over the swirl, then a light rumble of a diesel engine.

1847 HOURS (ART)

The light from the interior of the warehouse throws a long shadow onto the port.

The last crate has been loaded into two identical, black and yellow Buenos Aires taxi cabs.

Rafael has a horrible voice, but he loves to sing anyway.

"We sailed to the Canaries, to screw the local ladies, caught the crabs in Tenerife, the clap in Buenos Aires..."

Jeff loads the last gold bar into the second taxi.

"One more thing," adds Jeff.

He holds out a single velvet pouch with four large diamonds. "I took it from the boat. Thought it would make a great souvenir. Give them to our wives or maybe even a gift for Susan."

Rafael lights up. "Were you thinking about telling us at some stage?"

Jeff turns around. He is trying to keep his cool but won't take much more. "Watch your mouth, Rafa. This job isn't over yet."

Jeff hands out the diamonds, each taking an eight karat diamond in their sweaty hands. When done he holds the largest pink diamond up to the light.

Sergio is usually the quiet one but perks up. "That one's for Susan."

Rafael looks closely at Jeff. "I'd reckon she'd do every one of us for one of those."

Tulio breaks the standoff. "She got us the job. As far as I'm concerned, it would look good around her neck."

For a moment the tension dissolves. But only for a moment.

JANUARY 10, 0903 HOURS (ART)

The door opens and Jeff picks up the mail. As he does so he takes a quick glance down the street.

Tulio goes one way, Rafael the other. Jeff closes the front door. He leans down to tie his shoelace, takes out a matchbook and inserts it in the hinge. He locks the door and leaves.

Jeff's yellow and black Buenos Aires taxi is no more than a block away, parked on the square. Easy to see from all angles. He does a few walk-by's checking behind him. He checks the car once more before opening the door and entering.

Jeff revs up the Chrysler Hemi V8 and pulls out onto the highway. The taxi speeds around traffic and heads north towards el Tigre.

Jeff takes out his cell and pushes the contact pad. "We're back."

He can hear other voices in the background. Susan's voice is tense as if she has been waiting for a while. "What now?" she asks.

Jeff takes a right at the corner, drives by a passenger looking for a ride. He points up to the light which is permanently off duty.

"We lay low for a while. Then start fencing this stuff for real."

Susan is clearly pleased. "Come back in one piece. Oh and Jeff, I'll plan the party."

1505 HOURS (ART)

Outside, the heat is stifling and the traffic gridlocked but inside the King Fahd Mosque's thick marbled walls, the atmosphere is cool and secluded.

Emir Assad sits in a back room, sipping strong coffee, far away from the noises of the city.

A thin man in a dark suit walks forward and presents himself.

"Your name is Rami Sallum Mohammad," says Emir.

"Yes, sir."

The Emir, an expert on Muslim history, understands the irony. "Rami, the marksman." He takes a sip of the coffee. The Emir's voice is small and calming. "It is fitting."

"That is why I chose it," Sallum replies.

"You are familiar with the Koran?"

"Of course," Sallum replies.

"Then you will tell me the story of Hussain."

Sallum smiles. He circles his finger over the rim of his cup. "Hussain...the grandson of the prophet Mohammad, the third Imam?"

"That's him," says the Emir.

Sallum thinks for a second before beginning. "Killed by the Caliph Yazid in 680. The first of the great martyrs. His shrine in Karbala, Iraq is one of our holiest places."

The Emir pushes an old map over the table. It is an ancient map of Babylon and the Euphrates. "Tell me more."

The Emir points to the map; it spells out Fallujah.

Sallum continues. "The same place where the Infidel has met resistance. We defend it as we defend Allah."

The Emir walks over to the far wall and opens up a combination lock. From this hidden compartment he takes out a black suitcase and places it on the desk.

Sallum looks at it carefully. "My time has come."

"Those of us who fight for the faith must be prepared for martyrdom. It is this knowledge alone that gives us our advantage against the infidel."

2124 HOURS (ART)

The safe house looks sublime at night, shrouded in the diffused street lamp that illuminates half the street.

Tulio already has his keys in the door and begins to unlock the mechanism just as Jeff sees something that doesn't look right.

"Hold on."

He reaches down to see that his matchbook has been disturbed.

They look around at each other as Jeff slowly opens the door and shines a small ultraviolet light into the lobby.

The interior of the safe house is in complete darkness, the only illumination supplied by the streetlight outside.

Jeff points the U.V. light at a small laser trip wire that goes back to a black bundle that is firmly taped to the wall.

He looks over at Tulio who immediately knows what has to be done. "Get my day sack."

Tulio kneels down, avoiding the laser beam and spreads his hands lightly over the package. Jeff has the bag open and unzipped. They act as a team, practiced and smooth.

Tulio looks for the timing and power unit and finds the circuit board taped on top of what looks like TNT and C4 explosive. "I might be able to do this by hand."

"Might? Are you sure about it this time?"

Tulio thinks for a second. "I don't know, it could be a collapsible circuit."

Tulio looks back in disdain, wipes the sweat from his brow. "Got any better ideas?"

There is no answer, so he takes out his snips and looks for the positive and negative terminals. He takes a long look at the worried faces, then turns back to the work at hand. He holds his breath and makes the first cut.

Nothing.

He cuts the other terminal and folds back the wire.

2335 HOURS (ART)

The interior of the room remains tense and heated. All of the team stand around looking at what only a few minutes ago would have meant the end of their lives.

The bomb components are laid out on a white linen sheet, on the far right lies the main device.

Rafael picks up the grey package. "It could have taken off someone's legs."

He hands it to Jeff who weighs the package in his hands. "That would have made a statement."

Tulio inspects the mechanism. "We have two dets, one for back up—it's good work, doesn't look local."

"Has to be state sponsored. I don't know what you're thinking but we're in serious shit."

He cautiously pulls out a block of C4 which is affixed to a black box.

They stand back in awe.

Tulio looks at it closely then smiles to himself. "Awesome, it's Iranian. What the hell is that doing here?"

"Fuck knows. But we've got to find out who planted it. Next time we might not be so lucky."

JANUARY 11, 0147 HOURS (ART)

Gotan Tango, a sort of electronic version of the national song, plays on the radio. Jeff picks up his cell phone, begins to dial, and then clicks it closed.

He looks at the IED sitting on the floor. He hits redial. "Isa? Is that you?"

There is a pause on the line. Then her voice and she sounds enraged. "Jeff Tully. The man who is afraid of his own wedding?"

"Isabella, that's not fair."

"Fair? You try telling your father. That is brave. Not skipping town on some get rich quick plan."

"I was in trouble. If we're together, it might lead them to you."

"What kind of trouble?" Isa asks.

"It's for your own good, I can't explain now."

"Jeff. You said you were finished."

Jeff looks again at the IED. "I just wanted to hear your voice."

Jeff cups the receiver in his hand, despite their distance, he can feel her presence at the other end.

"I can't trust you. I don't know who you are anymore."Her tone hardens. "You think you can call and I jump back in your arms? I don't want to see you again."

She slams the phone down and Jeff stands there stunned, holding the phone in front of him. He takes a few moments before putting the receiver down.

0755 HOURS (ART)

It is a warm and humid morning as Jeff, Rafael and Sergio stroll across the main road. Argentines live a nocturnal life, dinner at 10:00pm and few are in bed before 3:00am. Hence, there are few people out at this time of the morning.

65

Cars swerve around a cartoñero who takes his time crossing the early traffic.

Jeff senses something. He looks up the street. Nothing but the sound of the squeaky wheels on the cartoñero's cart.

Then further up the street, a solitary vehicle. His suspicion falls on a Ford van that sits parked ahead, the condensation on the side windows blurring its contents. Then his eyes fix on the two shadows in the front. The Ford remains static, the old engine idles and sputters.

Jeff whispers into his headset: "Bravo. Two Tangos, heads up."

Covertly, he checks chamber in his HK 9 mm and nods to Rafael who holds up in a doorway.

The engine revs up and the driver pulls out. For a moment it's tires screech on the tarmac as it does a u-turn and begins to accelerate towards him.

Jeff runs to the other side of the road and drops behind a parked car.

The side door opens. Jeff pulls out the gun, clicks the safety off, tightens his trigger finger.

A package flies through the air and hits loudly against the kiosk wall. It is nothing but a bundle of newspapers.

Sergio shakes his head and pulls out the La Nacion newspaper from the bundle. He slaps a peso on the counter and crosses back over the road, looking carefully at the front page.

The van speeds away.

"They found the bodies," Sergio says.

"Where?" asks Jeff.

He unfolds the newspaper to show a headline and a grainy photo of bodies draped in white sheets.

Sergio translates from the Spanish headline: "Four floaters in the River Plate."

"Did they ID them?"

Sergio shakes his head as he dumps the paper in the trash bin.

1432 HOURS (ART)

The group sit in a bar with a few beers and peanuts. Tulio holds up his glass and looks at each of them.

"May we all live in interesting times."

The glasses clink as they finish their drinks.

Outside they encounter the San Telmo street market.

The central square is swarming with people, each looking for the next bargain. Silver pots, colored bottle siphons, bad paintings. Everything for sale. Jeff handles a pair of earrings and gestures to the stall owner, haggles with the price, hands it back.

Sergio walks beside him. "Never easy, buying for a woman."

Jeff looks at a few Baedeker books, sees the price and puts them down. "No way to tell what they like and don't like."

Sergio picks up something. "Think the wife might like this?" He holds up a gilded vase, overly ornate, frilly, conspicuous bad taste.

"For God's sake, no!"

Reluctantly, Sergio puts the piece down and they carry on walking. "Jeez, I kind of liked it." Sergio sulks along behind him.

"What's the rush anyway. We've got the rest of the week."

The throngs of Porteños, tourists, cops and locals fill the square. Tango musicians beat out the familiar rhythm, which echoes over the cobblestone walkways as it has done since the 1800's.

Jeff walks up to a bar. Through the window he spots Sergio who waits for a crowd of tourists to pass in front of him and then crosses the road.

Unexpectedly a Citroen swerves away from the curb, its tiny engine revs ferociously. Jeff looks back to Sergio but now a group of Japanese tourists block the view between them. The car heads directly for him, the speed increasing as it slams into his back.

Sergio flies forward and crashes into the bar window.

The crash of glass splays across the road, his body sprawls against the graffiti covered wood paneling. The car screeches to a halt abruptly, no more than 15 meters away. Backs up, wheels squealing violently.

Jeff dives onto Sergio, heaves him into the gutter, out of the corner of his eye he can see the wide tires of the grey Citroen.

Again the brake lights, the engine revs and the car speeds off.

Jeff rolls the two of them back to the sidewalk. Around them only shouts and screams of panic. For a moment the car is stationary and Jeff is close enough to look into the eyes of the driver.

The Citroen's tires slam hard into the curb as it makes a getaway. Sergio groggily opens his eyes.

"Che. Que passa?"

Jeff brushes the hair from his face. "Che, somebody just tried to kill you."

1814 HOURS (ART)

Back at the Palermo safe house, cigarette smoke fills the room. Sergio, wrapped up in gauze on his face and arms, sips from his mate gourd. The atmosphere is tense.

Jeff is the first to speak. "Anyway, we all saw it. I saw his eyes. They were different."

Tulio stubs out his cigarette. "What do you mean?"

"Not Porteño. Darker, Middle Eastern."

Rafael slams his fist on the table. He is shaking, as if the killer stands right before him. "I say we find him and kill him, now."

"Find him? Where? We don't have an ID, I didn't see a license, did you?" Jeff asks.

Tulio begins another cigarette. "First the bomb, now this. The question is, who would want to kill us?" He looks towards Sergio.

"Well?" Rafael asks.

Sergio pulls his head out of his hands. "I don't know. Anyway, nobody knows we're here."

"That leaves Al Qaeda. Maybe they are on to us."

69

"How? We killed everyone on board. They've probably only just discovered the money's missing."

Tulio takes a long drag. "Maybe it's local."

Rafael looks up as the smoke escapes through the open window. "How about the fence, does he know something?"

"No, why?"

Rafael turns against Tulio. He stabs his finger into his chest. "He's a fucking bandito, isn't he? He knows we just swiped fifty million, maybe he figures he'll take it himself."

But Tulio keeps his cool. He shakes his head. "Boludos. There's an honor among crooks. Banditos have it too. Anyway, like I said, they don't know where we are."

Tulio attempts to hide his anger despite Rafael's accusation. But when accusation flows freely it can become contagious. One by one they begin to look at each other as potential enemies. They keep silent as they work out the possibilities.

Sergio is the first. He nods towards Rafael. "I saw him. He talked to someone."

Jeff looks over at Rafael. "Well?"

Rafael tries to recollect. "Okay, I called home. The wife and kids."

Jeff can't believe it. "Shit, this is not happening. We all agreed, no contacts. "

Rafael acts as if it is nothing. "A text message. I called her back, that's all."

Jeff has heard enough. He motions for the cell phone which Rafael produces from his pocket. Jeff takes the cheap Nokia and crushes it with his boot.

"That goes for all of you!" he says. He walks around the table looks at each of them. "There's only one thing to do."

Rafael tries to put the pieces of his Nokia together before giving up. "What's that?"

"Whoever it is, they know where we are. So we sit up and wait. Let them come to us."

JANUARY 12, 1115 HOURS (ART)

Emir Assad walks slowly between the shopping aisles. The Saffaud Mercado in the La Boca barrio of Buenos Aires is a typical Arabian deli, catering to their own people, selling halal meats, mint teas and sweets.

"Salam alaikum. You are well, my brother?"

Sallum looks a little subdued. "I am well, sahib."

"You have sowed fear among the enemy. We are proud of what you accomplished. The operation continues."

Sallum bows his head modestly as the Emir continues:

"But we have decided to speed up our priorities."

Sallum looks around the bare room. A copy of the Buenos Aires Herald sits on the desk, next to a picture of his wife and child.

The Emir is on a roll. "Every revolution experiences defeat as well as victory."

Sallum's eyebrows twitch. "A defeat, sahib?"

71

"Our shipment attacked. Everything on board stolen, brothers killed."

Sallum fingers the thin, six inch dagger that sits in his jacket pocket. "No one would dare. Not against Al Qaeda."

"You are wrong. "

He lays out four black and white photos on the desk. "Now you will make them pay."

Sallum picks up the photos. A smile appears across his face as he stares at them one by one.

1145 HOURS (ART)

The Faena Hotel is full of new arrivals, hoping to find their rooms ready for occupation after the long flight down to South America.

Upstairs, the team sit nervously awaiting their next orders.

Jeff checks the windows and peeks through the curtains down to the courtyard below. He paces nervously. From the look of the argument coming from the front desk, the new arrivals were going to have to wait.

There is a knock on the door. Jeff glances at Rafael who pulls out a 9mm HK, stands behind the door.

On the second knock, Jeff opens the door.

Susan enters. She wears a dark suit with a white, open necked shirt; a thin string of pearls hangs around her neck. She glances at Jeff briefly, then looks around the room and the rest of the team. Jeff sees a crease on her brow, a cold, suspicious look.

Susan breaks into a smile. "I have it from the top, you've achieved a significant blow against Al Qaeda.

Without money, they are finished. Congratulations, boys."

Tulio lets out a cry and there are cheers all around.

Susan motions for quiet. "As far as I know there's no change of plan."

Jeff looks at the other faces. "Try telling that to Serge. Someone tried to kill him."

"When?"

Rafael is the first to answer. "Yesterday, San Telmo market."

Jeff turns towards Susan. "Then there's the little matter of an IED planted inside our safe house. Something's going on and we want to know."

Jeff plants a block of C4 on the table. Susan looks at it for a few seconds then puts it in her purse. She surveys the room then takes Jeff aside and lowers her voice.

"Look, Jeff, I can run some tests but this might not be related. The Porteños have had it tough since the economic collapse. Somebody might have heard something. You know how these things are."

"We're more worried about Al Qaeda."

Susan brushes against his arm. "Yes, I can understand. And none of you have been shooting your mouths off?"

Rafael appears behind them. "We're quite sure."

"Maybe a local bandito knows something and is trying to score big. How the hell do I know?"

"We've laid low, behaved ourselves."

Susan turns away and searches inside her purse. She places a digital recorder on the table and presses the play button.

A scared Arabic voice screams through the airwaves, the fear is burnt into the tone of his voice until the signal goes dead.

Susan switches it off.

"The captain's last minutes. He made a call on a sat phone. We had it translated. He's telling his controller that the boat's been hit, he needs back up. After the charge exploded, I guess it took the sat phone with it."

Susan looks at the men, one by one. "The NSA monitors most satellite transmissions down here. Especially since Al Qaeda moved in." She looks up to see that the mood in the room has become significantly edgier. "The fact is that if you had bagged them right away, this wouldn't have happened."

Most of them shrug it off but Rafael is offended. "Easy to say. You weren't there."

Susan just shrugs her shoulders. "Well, I'm not sure it's that important. They would have found out at one stage. It doesn't say who you are, what you look like, or more importantly, where you are."

"But it tells us that Al Qaeda are on to us earlier than we thought," Jeff adds.

Susan brushes this off. "Either way, it's of no concern to the Agency. The job's done—we move on."

As Susan stands up to leave she turns towards the door as Rafael slips the recorder into his pocket.

Jeff has one more request. "We risked our lives. The least you can do is give us some protection."

Susan sneers as she stares him down. "How soon you forget, Jeff. This job was off the books, never official."

Susan turns on her heels. "Hasta luego."

1431 HOURS (ART)

The interior of the Cafe Tortoni is full of tourists as usual.

Sallum and Emir look a little out of place among the other orders of cocktails, Malbec wine and loud voices.

"Let me try to understand," Sallum asks. "The CIA organize a hit on our boat. Then pass it on to their source in the mosque here, who they know is a double agent. Am I close?"

"So far," the Emir answers cryptically.

"He tells us the names, where they are hiding and you send me in."

"Clever, you have to admit."

Sallum looks over at a young American couple, exchanging a long kiss. He is instantly disgusted. Something doesn't sit right in his mind. "But why would they do it?"

The Emir takes a sip of his coffee. "Because they want me, they want the cell. They don't care for their own, never have."

Sallum thinks about this for a moment. "If I give my life, I do it with honor."

"Look, they cannot be allowed to steal from Al Qaeda. I have faith in you, we all must have faith in the prophet in these times of struggle."

A glaze forms over Sallum's eyes. "The wisdom of the master."

The Emir knows he has found his man. "I can feel it, the moment of victory is close."

1635 HOURS (ART)

Back at the Palermo safe house, Jeff checks his gun, loads the magazine. He clicks the bolt, releases the safety. "She said no safe house, so this will be it. We've got no choice but to lay low, stay in the clear."

Tulio dials in the numbers. The lock on the safe is an old Meyer model. "We can use some money to change names, new passports, credit cards. We can always disappear."

Jeff agrees. "We hold out for a week and we'll be safe."

Sergio jumps up and starts to walk back and forth. "What's with you?"

"Maybe you've forgotten. I have a wife and kids."

Jeff doesn't want to hear it. "Out of the question."

"They need me," Sergio persists.

"Sergio, we had an agreement."

Sergio grabs his jacket and heads for the door. He has clearly made up his mind. "I'm a Porteño, I don't need to hide like you."

2212 HOURS (ART)

The team have set up a guard house, perched atop the safe house. There is a lookout at the top of the water tower which holds the house water supply. Every angle can be controlled from this perspective.

Rafael braces his back against the water tank and holds the scope steady. He takes a shallow breath and pans the scope in a wide arc across the street.

It steadies on a dark shadow, a man in a doorway, his breath barely visible in the balmy night. Suddenly Tulio appears and embraces the stranger.

Rafael is distracted by the sound of footsteps on the wrought iron spiral staircase.

"Anything interesting?" It is Sergio, come to relieve him of guard duty.

Sergio taps him on the shoulder and Rafael leaves the gun in place, starts to descend the stairs.

Rafael turns back to face Sergio. "Keep an eye on him. That faggot is up to something, I know it."

Sergio hands the scope to Rafael and takes hold of the gun.

Rafael looks closely as Tulio and the Shadow discuss something and then vanish inside the building.

JANUARY 13, 0945 HOURS (ART)

Jeff veers past a large group of loud tourists. He makes for the back of the bar, for the rear room where the pool tables sit unused. In the corner he sees a woman siting, a copy of El Nacion in her hands. On the cover, the photo of dead bodies and a grainy image of what looks like Sergio.

Susan is all business this morning as she folds up the newspaper and places it in front of her coffee. "We ran the tests, Langley says it's Iranian. "

She places the block of plastic in his hand. "And I tried to find another safe house. They wouldn't listen."

77

"Don't lie, Susan. The Agency has plenty of safe houses, even in this part of the world."

Susan moves the newspaper closer to him. Close enough for him to smell the perfume on her neck. "You don't get the type of pressure I'm under. Something big is going down. Intel tells us they've been training down here. They'll move up to the forbidden zone and then up to the border with Mexico. Then it's just a short hop up the East Coast."

"What's the target?"

"DC, Congress and the Senate, but it's anyone's guess. Look, we are grateful for what you guys have done. In a calmer time we'd be able to help, but..."

"Don't worry, we're big boys, we'll survive." He can feel her hand lingering on his knee. Jeff continues, ignoring her. "Sergio had to go back to his family, there was nothing I could do."

She pulls her hand off instantly. "You should have stayed together. A good team always sticks together. What about the others?"

"Sitting tight, waiting for things to die down."

Susan smiles at him. "Let me know where you are. If there's anything I can do..."

"Thanks."

She moves to leave, but then stops and turns back. "One other thing," she says. "My recorder."

"What about it?"

"Did you take it?"

Jeff holds up his hands. "Are accusing me now?"

"No, just asking."

"Sure you didn't lose it?"

"Quite sure."

Jeff stares into her blue eyes. "I'll ask around."

He fishes around in his jeans pocket. Eventually he finds what he is looking for; the diamond is still wrapped in tissue paper. He places it on the table and pushes it towards her. He waits for a few seconds for her to unwrap it.

Susan takes out the gem and holds it up to the chandelier. "My own Al Qaeda diamond. Thank you, Jeff. I'll have it set in gold, made into a necklace to remember this by."

The diamond is cut in a hexagonal pattern, tiny beads of light reflect off her eyes.

Susan looks at him as he begins to study the newspaper. "Jeff, when I wear it, I'll think of you."

1753 HOURS (ART)

Back at the Palermo safe house, the team are guarding against any form of attack.

Sergio talks quietly on his cell—his gun sight pans the street. Boredom has begun to set in. Rafael still pores over the Crusades book as Sergio slurps his yerba mate through a metal straw.

Rafael wears a disgusted expression. "What's with you people down here? I can't believe you drink that shit."

"What can I say? It calms me down. Try some, you might actually like it." Sergio takes another sip.

"Ah, stop it! That's disgusting."

He spits it out. Sergio laughs out loud. "It's an acquired taste, much like your alcohol. What's that?" He points to the book.

Rafael slams the book shut. "The Crusades."

"Still reading that historical crap?"

"Man, it's not crap. Listen." He begins to read and Sergio actually listens. "Many of the old crusader forts in Palestine are still used to this day. In 1982 the fortress of Beaufort was besieged by General Ariel Sharon just as the great Arab leader Saladin had done nine centuries before. In May of 2000, the Israelis evacuated the fortress as the Crusaders had done back in 1187, before the fall of Jerusalem."

Jeff enters the room. "Who cares, Rafael? It's still ancient history."

The computer screen pings and Jeff and Rafael look at the screen.

Jeff grabs his jacket. "Looks like she has something."

1945 HOURS (ART)

In a Palermo pool hall Susan shoots a solid into the corner pocket. "Buenos Aires, 1994, Israeli Embassy."

An open pack of cigarettes and empty rounds of brandy glasses perch off the rim of the pool table.

"Before my time," says Jeff. "Was that the terrorist bombing?"

"Yes. Another Iranian connection. We put it down to their work with Odessa. Ring a bell?"

"Not really." Jeff takes a shot and misses.

Susan stands and takes her cue. "My German isn't that good but it stands for Organisation der ehemaligen SS-Angehörigen...Odessa."

Jeff stops in his tracks. "Nazis?"

"Yes. There's plenty of them down here. Escapees from World War Two and their descendants."

Jeff leans on his cue, he has suddenly lost all interest in the game. "You think they could be working with Al Qaeda?"

"It's just a theory. I wouldn't bet against it."

Jeff takes his cue and stares towards the cafe.

Susan studies him in deep thought. "What's on your mind?"

He shakes it off and hits a red in the corner pocket. "Maybe I'm coming to terms with the insanity of all of this."

JANUARY 14, 0525 HOURS (ART)

Dawn is starting to break, the sun rises over the cobblestones sending shafts of bright orange light from the east.

Sallum sits behind the wheel of his Mercedes 300SL. He has been here for some time now, the heat from the engine long gone, condensation from his breath starts to form on the windshield.

He waits patiently.

0732 HOURS (ART)

Sergio closes the ornate front door, looks left and right and starts walking. He turns towards the square where the shops are just opening up. Trucks line the

81

alley, men loading crates of vegetables and huge carcasses of meat through the side doors.

A mongrel, looking for food, pounces out in front of him. Sergio ignores the dog and heads across the square to the taxi stand.

0752 HOURS (ART)

Sallum follows Sergio along the La Boca avenue. He pulls up the collar of his long grey overcoat, crosses the street to the taxi stand and approaches Sergio who has just put down the call phone and waits patiently for the taxi.

"Excuse me, do you know the way to San Telmo?"

Sergio looks up surprised. "Head back up the street, turn left. You can't miss it."

"Is it far?" the dark stranger asks.

The three legged mongrel has returned, sniffing around ankles, looking for scraps of food.

"Not far, maybe ten minutes."

Sallum kneels down to pat the dog. Within that split second of distraction he pulls a Walther P7 from his pocket and levels it at Sergio. In one move he grabs his arm and jams the pistol into the side of his chest.

Sallum's voice is calm.

"Not a word. Walk back towards the house."

They walk slowly for a few yards. Behind them, the taxi has arrived, the cabbie looks up and down the street for his fare.

Sergio stands in front of the door. He waits for a second until he feels the jab of the gun in his back. Sergio takes his keys, opens the door. Inside they can hear

82

the sound of a child playing followed by a woman's voice.

Sallum pushes Sergio into the entrance hall.

Sergio shouts down the hallway: "Cariño correr! Tomar el niño, correr!"

Sallum grabs Sergio's head and jerks it back hard. "Shut up! You'll only make things worse."

He pulls back the hammer, presses the gun barrel against his throat and pushes Sergio forward along the hall. The wife and child freeze as they see their husband and father pushed into the room.

Sallum makes the wife and child sit on the sofa. He stands in front of them. "Do exactly what I say and no one gets hurt."

Sergio makes the mistake of shouting again: "Don't do it, cariño. Es mentira, cabron!"

This time Sallum shoves Sergio hard against the wall. Plates crash on the kitchen floor.

The wife screams, the boy cries and Sergio takes his chance. He lunges at Sallum, fist raised, muscles clenched.

But Sallum has anticipated the move. He swivels and ducks, delicate moves like a well-trained fighter. He catches the back of Sergio's fist, pushes the P7 into the soft flesh of his palm and fires.

Blood splatters on the wall. Sergio doubles over in pain, then tries desperately to stop the flow of blood. Sallum follows this with a swift blow to the chin. The blow sends Sergio to the floor. Sallum adds a kick to the head and Sergio lies unconscious.

Sallum looks at the wife as she trembles on the sofa. "I can be reasonable. Do what I say, you won't be hurt."

He throws a pair of plastic cuffs on the floor next to Sergio's motionless body. "Cuff him...and shut that one up."

She shakes her head. Swiftly, he grabs the boy, who looks nervously at his father, then his mother.

"Do what I say. Tie him!"

She takes the cuffs and places them affectionately around Sergio's wrist, wipes the sweat from his brow and kisses him gently. "What do you want?"

He shakes his head as he takes off his black rucksack. He opens up a mini tripod and takes out a camcorder. He looks again at the boy who now clings to the side of his mother. He takes out a small vial of smelling salts and passes them under Sergio's nose.

Sallum looks into Sergio's dazed eyes. "Sit very still."

Sergio's eyes are bloodshot but his pupils move from right to left as he rapidly regains consciousness.

Sallum is pleased with the process. "Now, come here," he says to the wife. "Slowly."

Sergio's wife looks at her husband, then back towards Sallum who immediately detects her defiance.

"Now!" Sallum shouts this time.

Nervously she freezes in place. Sallum levels the P7 at her head, squeezes the trigger.

Thud!

The bullet strikes her in the forehead, her body falls back against the sofa. Sallum walks towards her, shoves the gun in her mouth and fires another bullet. Her body sails back, jerks once then lies still.

Sallum kneels down on the floor next to Sergio. "A quick death. She is very lucky."

He reaches for his rucksack and pulls out a white card with something written on it. He passes it to Sergio. "Read it."

Sergio looks back in defiance. "Cabron!"

"Read it to the camera. Now!"

"You'll kill me anyway."

Sallum thinks for a moment. "Yes. But I don't have to kill the boy."

Sergio looks over at his son who is leaning over his mother, tears flowing down his cheeks. "What kind of human are you?"

Sallum pulls out a black ski mask and puts it on.

A grainy image appears on the small television.

"You know better than to steal from al Qaeda. You should have known what the punishment must be."

Sergio glances at the piece of paper. He shakes his head.

"You will do it."

Sergio's mouth begins to shake as he makes out the words.

Sallum is checking the monitor. "Look up at the camera and speak clearly."

Again Sergio looks into his eyes, sees the hatred, there is no way out. He stares into the camera.

Sallum is still checking the effect. "Look straight in. I want your friends to see your eyes."

85

Sergio begins to speak, his voice broken and defeated: "You should not steal from Al Qaeda. I am getting what I deserve and you will get it, too. If you give back the money and turn yourself in, they'll just kill you but leave your families. Do it, boys, it's not worth it. You've seen what happened to me."

Sallum switches the camera off and lines up the barrel of the P7.

JANUARY 15, 0745 HOURS (ART)

The safe house is filled with grunts and groans. The grainy image is darkly lit and pixilated, but the point is brought home.

Jeff watches the monitor as the handgun is lined up with Sergio's face, the distorted scream fills the tense stillness of the room, the camera runs for a while and then only white noise as the tape comes to an end. He stands up and switches it off.

Rafael turns to him. "How did you get it?"

Jeff ejects the DVD. "Came in the mail this morning."

"The murdering bastard! The same one who tried to blow us to kingdom come."

"We'll find him."

Tulio has been watching from afar. "Unless he finds us first."

"Who the fuck is he?" asks Rafael.

Tulio is first to answer. "A professional. Look at the mask and gloves, no way we can ID him."

Jeff places the DVD back in the envelope. "So what's the video for?"

Rafael laughs. "To scare the shit out of us!"

A tense silence for a second as they know it has succeeded.

Jeff is the first to talk. "Sergio goes home and within a day he's dead. How can that happen unless they know exactly who he is and where to find him?"

"The most obvious answer is someone told him—maybe someone in this room."

Jeff turns towards Tulio. "Now why the fuck would anyone do that?"

Tulio is packing his bag. "A big heist, split four ways that's seven and a half million each. Now one of us is dead and suddenly we're splitting it three ways, ten mil each. Sounds like a motive to me."

Rafael turns towards him, fire in his eyes. "There's only one person who would do that. A lying Gaucho bastard like you!"

Jeff stands between them. "Cool it, all of you! Are we going to do their work for them?"

Tulio steps back, his face sullen. "Cabron! If it was me, why would I raise the issue? Why would I point the finger at myself?"

He strides away, disgusted with the whole lot of them.

1005 HOURS (ART)

The morning sun shines through the safe house's shutters and casts a long shadow on the huge kitchen.

Rafael enters and pours himself a coffee. He joins Jeff at the long table. "You still trust him?"

Jeff takes a sip of his coffee. "With my life. I know him and his family, he's been like a brother to me."

Rafael looks around the room. "So what now?"

Jeff takes off the kettle and swirls the water around, before dumping the contents down the drain.

"It's not me...and it's not you. We go back to Pendleton and beyond. It's not Tulio, but then again he's from up north, Susan said something about an Al Qaeda cell up there. "

Rafael cannot believe what he's hearing. "What are you saying?"

Jeff holds his head in his hands. "I don't know anymore. Maybe I should never have let him in..."

Rafael suddenly turns cold."Maybe we should just fuck him over—make him talk."

1642 HOURS (ART)

A taxi swerves through the lanes of Avenue Libertador, the wide avenue that flows from east to west through the city.

Inside the taxi, Jeff takes out his cellular.

Isabella answers on the first ring, she knows it's him. "Where are you, Jeff?"

Jeff cups the phone. "Can't say over the phone. Just wanted to hear your voice."

Isabella is at once suspicious."What's going on, Jeff? What are you up to?"

"Work, that's all," he answers. "Security stuff—things have hit a rough patch. I need a few days to sort it out."

He doesn't need to see her face to know that she is confused and angry.

Isabella hesitates. Then: "There were some people here, watching the house..."

"When? What did they look like?" She can hear the concern in his voice.

"Walking home the other night from the club, two of them. They seemed friendly, asked about you. Nothing more."

"Isabella, listen to me. Anyone who approaches you in the next few days, stay out of their way."

"What's happening, Jeff?"

Jeff hesitates. Then: "Just be careful. Everything will be okay. Trust me."

2137 HOURS (ART)

The Palermo streets are particularly humid tonight as Jeff walks alone towards the safe house.

Out of the corner of his eye he notices a car approaching. The headlights skim over his face as he ducks into an alley, pulls his gun, and waits for the car to pass. Nothing extraordinary, so he places the gun back behind the waistband of his jeans.

He steps back out into the street only to feel a sharp prod in his back, a gun.

Sallum holds the barrel sharply against his back.

"Keep walking."

Sallum leads him for a while and then halts at a black Mercedes.

Sallum pushes him against the door.

"Your weapon. No sudden moves, you know what I'm capable of."

Jeff places the HK 9mm onto the driver's seat as he gets into the car.

Sallum shoves his gun tightly into Jeff's ribs and searches his body.

"Place the other weapons on the dash, starting with the knife."

Jeff calmly complies, first the knife in his pocket, then the tiny four-shot revolver tucked into his boot.

Sallum is eventually convinced that he is disarmed. "Okay, you drive."

The interior of the old Mercedes is clean and well oiled. Jeff takes a brief look around to familiarize himself with the controls.

He clicks his seat belt and notices Sallum is too concerned to put his on. He revs the big German V8 and accelerates away.

2152 HOURS (ART)

The car drives through the boulevards, around the obelisk and the gaudy lingerie billboards that light the way out of the city.

Sallum looks over at Jeff. He releases the pressure from the gun.

Jeff turns right onto the main road that leads exits the city. "So, how did you end up like this?"

Sallum sneers as he looks out the window. The huge Telefonica billboard buzzes by. "Afghanistan. Didn't you guess?"

Jeff pushes the accelerator, the roads are thin at this time of night. Within a few seconds he is up to the speed limit. "You haven't told me how it all began."

Sallum checks the gun's chamber. "My father was mujahideen, a lieutenant of Ahmad Shah Massoud."

Jeff seems to have some recollection. "The Lion of Panjshir?"

Jeff follows Sallum's hand signals. A few minutes later he turns off the carretera onto the 175 that runs north to El Tigre.

Sallum continues. "It started at the American school in Kabul, thought I'd get the life he never had."

"What happened?"

Sallum crunches his eyes up, putting himself back in his own shoes. "First the Taliban came."

"Financed by our government?"

"Yes, your CIA."

Jeff notices the ring road for the Tigre Delta and carries on along the carretera.

"The school, was it madrassah?"

Sallum nods his head slowly as they enter the beginning of a work zone, but it is night, no one is around.

Jeff has seen the oncoming traffic signs and slows to the allowable speed, around 70KPH. Sallum continues talking, he is now deep into an emotional, sub conscious state. Jeff continues changes down a gear.

Sallum continues. "We did not think the war would come to us, we thought it was for the cities: Kabul, Kandahar. Once there had been a camp by my village but no one knew what went on there."

Jeff looks over at Sallum. "You never thought that you could be a target?"

Sallum rubs his temples as if he has the world's worst headache. "Why exactly do you care?"

Jeff looks in the mirror but the road is still empty. "Nothing, just figured we're both soldiers. We have that in common."

Sallum continues. "I had drawn water from the well, told my wife when I'd be home from the city. It was like any other day...one by one I said goodbye to them."

Jeff spots his chance; a work zone, barely 200 meters ahead.

Sallum stares ahead but seems to not see the red cones and heavy equipment on the side of the road. "God forgive me for I talked sharply to my wife, told her: 'Clean up the house, it looks like a pigsty'!"

A pile of sand dumped only yards off to the side of the road. Jeff sees his chance and nods his head as if he is listening. He heads for it.

Sallum continues in a monotone. "I drove past the mosque where I had prayed every day. Nothing had changed, it was a regular day."

Sallum winces as he relives the gruesome moment. The sudden increase in revs is barely audible inside the old Mercedes. "Suddenly, I don't know why, I looked up and saw the trails in the sky."

FLASHBACK
Sallum can see the contrail high above in the sky.

He is back in Afghanistan, it is a day like any other. A thin white line slices through the pale blue, midday sky. A thin contrail across a cloudless mountain sky followed by the thunder of a US Air Force jet.

Sallum looks into the rear view mirror of his beat up Nissan pickup. Behind him he see a small cloud forming behind the village, the plumes of smoke rising above the mountains and into the peaceful sky.

END FLASHBACK

As the cones get closer, Jeff floors the accelerator and steers the car directly towards the pile of sand.

The car slams into it.

Sallum has barely a second to react before the collision. He braces his body but without any seatbelt to hold him he shoots through the windshield. His limp body flies through the air, deep into the darkness and finally comes to rest on a pile of sand.

Back in the car, Jeff can hear the ticking of the hot engine and feel the pain of the seat belt tugging against his chest. He feels around in the back for a weapon and grabs it. A Makharov 9mm automatic.

Quickly he exits the car and looks around, listening to the crickets chirping in the night.

He makes a cursory search in front of the smoking Mercedes. But there is no sign of Sallum, only a pool of blood and footprints that trail off into the brush. For a moment he thinks he hears movement in the still night but he is alone and dazed, the car a total wreck.

He turns and jogs back towards El Tigre.

JANUARY 16, 0237 HOURS (ART)

At the safe house, Rafael applies antiseptic cream to Jeff's head and bandages the cut above his eye. Jeff's cellular rings.

Rafael looks at his fixed eyes. "Are you going to answer?"

Jeff flips the button. "Hola?"

A male voice: "Well, are we on?"

Jeff mouths to Rafael: "Raul" Then, back into the phone: "Yes. Everything has been arranged."

There is a pause on the line. "Has something gone wrong?" Raul asks.

Jeff winces as Rafael applies an alcohol swab to the open wound. "It's worth fifty million, we'll sell it for thirty. That's all you need to know. And I'll make the drop-off, not Tulio."

Jeff cuts the cell phone. He stands and approaches the card table.

Rafael is all ready with his question. "So, how did he find us?"

"I emailed the cell number."

Rafael is not pleased by another breach of protocol. "They could have intercepted it."

Jeff throws the phone onto the table. "Fuck it, I know. How else can we make the exchange? We have to talk to someone, right?"

Rafael cleans up the first aid kit. "Maybe they'll wait until we hand it over then take us down. There's bound to be more of them than us."

Jeff looks at the phone, there's no fixing it. "I told you, there's nothing safe about this mission. Now, if we want the cash we have to take a few chances."

Rafael stands above him. "Who says we need to go and pick up the money? Why not have the fence stash it for us."

Jeff laughs out loud. "Are you kidding? This is Argentina!"

But Rafael remains serious. "Wait until we've smoked the murderer, then go collect."

Jeff dismisses it. "Look, someone has to be there when the exchange goes down. And it has to be one of us."

Rafael thinks about this for a while."If you don't show by tomorrow, I'm not paying for it with my life."

Jeff stands. "Sure, if that's what you want. But I'll be there at Retiro station. From there we all go our own ways."

But Rafael is not finished. "What about Tulio? Notice he's never around?"

Jeff stands perfectly still, frozen as if he were a block of ice. "What the hell are you saying, Rafi?"

"Neat and convenient, isn't it? You're the one who puts it all together, pulls all the strings. Sergio, now Tulio. Maybe he's dead."

Jeff slaps Rafael across the face. Rafael falls back, shocked for a brief second. He wipes the thin trickle of blood from his mouth.

"They were my friends, too," Jeff says.

Rafael charges forward.

His fist rams into Jeff's stomach. Jeff doubles up in pain, chokes on his own breath. He pulls himself upright and swings his fist backward, but it misses.

Both of them are disturbed by the sound of a door closing and footsteps echoing along the hall.

Susan stands motionless above them. "You idiots, what do you think you are doing?"

Jeff stares up at Rafael, shocked by the sudden intrusion.

Rafael turns his attention back to Jeff. "So prove it. You weren't with Sergio when he was killed?"

Jeff stands and brushes himself off. "It's ridiculous. If I was going to kill you I'd have done it by now."

A sullen grin appears on his lips as he slams the door behind him and grabs his keys..

1317 HOURS (ART)

The old diesel commuter train rattles along the tracks towards El Tigre.

Jeff looks out the window at one of the many 'Villa Miserias'—the slums at the outskirts of Buenos Aires. He smokes a cigarette, sits somewhere towards the back of the train, where he can keep an eye on the front carriages.

He is alone, finally. Time to think about the last few days.

He peers out of the window, the shanty towns are a wash of rusted corrugated iron, rotten stucco and broken terra-cotta tiles.

Jeff jumps out of the train and makes for the kiosk. He orders a choripán, a sausage sandwich. As he pays the cook, he notices his hands shaking. He takes a bite of the sandwich but suddenly his appetite has gone and throws it in the garbage. He walks to the exit.

1410 HOURS (ART)

The El Tigre bar is full for a change.

Jeff checks the entrance once again. His eyes wander around the room. Nothing out of the ordinary, he walks over to the office, tries to relax.

A man enters behind him, walks over to the bar and orders a beer. He unfolds a copy of the Buenos Aires Herald and begins reading. He is a stout man, early forties, almost six feet tall, rare for a Porteño. He wears a black suit, a blue cotton shirt with a few buttons undone to show his carefully groomed chest. Jeff moves a little closer.

The man looks up.

"You look like shit. Order a steak with chimichurri, it's the special for today. It might put some meat on your bones."

Jeff takes a look at the menu, then places it down on the bar. "Let's get one thing straight, Raul. People are getting killed. I'm probably next."

Raul takes a sip of his beer. "I'm sorry to hear about Tulio."

"We haven't found a body yet but we can assume the worst. How well did you know him?"

"In this trade you never know anyone too well."

Jeff seems pleased with the response and takes a long sip of his beer. "Look, El Madryn arrives at 1:45

am. We make the exchange at midnight, when the nightlife gets going. It will be easier then."

Raul passes over the ledger and Jeff takes a close look. "Thirty million, agreed?"

"Sure. The money is ready," Raul answers.

Jeff looks around, suddenly nervous. "Where?"

Raul smiles briefly. "In a safe place."

"So, how does it work?"

"Just get your stuff, bring it to me. I have it authenticated, you get the cash. Quite simple really."

"How do I know I won't be face up in the Rio de la Plata by the day's end?"

Raul looks out at the river and lights up a thin cigar. "Mutual trust. It's what makes our world turn."

He smiles from ear to ear as he takes the ledger and heads out onto the street.

1613 HOURS (ART)

The cool breeze of the Andes mountains flow down to the valley floor.

Isabella sits at her laptop and stares out the window. She smiles at what she sees; the blurry outlines of two figures riding on horseback. It is her brother Tulio and her father, roping a stallion.

The chirping comes from her laptop and she is brought back to the present. She clicks into the instant message.

"Isa, is that you?"

There is a pause as she looks at the screen, not knowing what to do.

"You don't want to hear it, but I..."

Tears drop onto Isabella's laptop.

"I've been thinking. I just want to be with you the rest of my life. I know I don't have any music and I don't have any favorite readings. In fact I don't have much of anything. But I want to go through with it."

Isabella begins to type in some letters.

She begins to type, "I miss y..."

But then she stops.

Slowly she erases the letters and closes the laptop.

JANUARY 17, 0115 HOURS (ART)

At the El Tigre docks a huge crane dangles containers like toys in the air. Everything is automated, row upon row of produce and cargo containers spread to the edge of the dark muddy waters of the Rio de la Plata.

Jeff points up to a rusted container that has a faded star and the letters "ARM" stenciled on the corrugated side. "That's it."

Raul snaps to attention and looks up. The crane hoists the single steel walled container off the boat. Metal screeches as the crane adjusts the heavy weight, then the ropes tighten to winch the container onto the dock.

An obese man walks towards them. "Biletto?"

Jeff takes the receipt from his briefcase and hands it over. The manager inspects it briefly then points a light into his face.

"Documentos?"

Jeff hands over his ID and the manager inspects it closely. Jeff's eyes don't leave the ID as he reaches inside his coat, slips the safety off the HK 9mm.

99

The port manager checks his face again, opens an ancient laptop and places the photo over the scanner.

Jeff hands over the manifest. The manager looks over the frames of his eye glasses. He opens the piece of paper and sees the dollar bills inside. He counts out the first five one hundred dollar bills and folds them neatly in his pocket.

0125 HOURS (ART)

A few minutes later, the container smashes onto the back of the ancient Ford truck.

Jeff hops into the passenger's seat as Raul drives the truck forward into the parking lot. From the corner of his eye, Jeff can see the Customs Inspector approaching.

Raul places his hand on Jeff's shoulder. "Okay, now let me do the talking."

The Inspector takes a cursory walk around the container and checks the paperwork. "Destino?"

"Palermo," Raul answers.

"Contenidos?"

"Chatarra, hiero, acero, algo de plomo," Raul answers soundly, making sure to keep his eyes forward.

The inspector passes his hand across the container's outside skin and points his flashlight once more into their eyes. He holds it there for what seems like an eternity but is probably no more than a few seconds. He walks again towards the rear of the container and checks that the numbers match the bill of lading. Finally he tosses the documents into Jeff's lap and waves the truck through.

"What was that all about back there?"

"I told him it was full of scrap metal, steel and a bit of lead. He bought it, too."

The truck comes to a halt beside a thicket of trees, only a few outbuildings visible.

Jeff steps down from the truck, followed closely by Raul. In the distance a branch cracks. He draws his gun, sweeps the semi darkness ahead.

"Still nervous?" Raul asks.

Jeff slips the gun back in his waistband. "We've already lost two, I don't plan on being the third."

Raul slides the steel gate to the side and Jeff follows behind. Inside, there are several vehicles lined up against the far wall.

Raul kneels down, reaches under the first vehicle. He finds a catch, releases it and the flat metal panel comes free in his hand. Where the bottom of a car usually is, there are rows of wooden boxes. Raul pulls the first one free and hands it to Jeff.

Banknotes; Euros, Dollars, Swiss Francs.

The container is opened to reveal two wooden crates. Raul takes a crowbar and pries back the side. The diamonds sparkle back at him, clear as the eyes of a newborn child.

Raul's face can barely hide the excitement. "Conyo! Where did you get these beauties?"

Raul pulls up a gold bar, turns it over to read the mark: A.Q. and a crescent.

Raul whistles through his teeth. "You're a brave man, Jeff Tully."

"No, just desperate."

Raul holds up a scope and examines the quality of the diamonds. "Within thirty-six hours, we split it up a hundred ways. Within a week it will be in a thousand different jewelers in a dozen different countries. You can relax now my friend."

"Right. Just don't fault me if I worry."

Raul pats him on the back. "It's just the reality of gold and diamonds. Not the way they sparkle and glitter, or the way that women flock to their beauty. But the fact that they are untraceable. Nobody cares where they come from as long as they are real."

Raul stands back and opens two huge duffel bags.

0535 HOURS (ART)

Jeff does a walk by on the safe house. Nothing out of the ordinary, he feels for the key but it's not where he left it. He pulls out his gun, holds it out before him. He senses a slight movement behind him.

He is pushed away, a leg slammed into his gut. He look down a barrel of a gun pointed straight at his head.

"He was alive this morning. Only one of us knew where he was."

Jeff swings around, kicks his leg into Rafael's gut— he crumples to the floor. Jeff takes out the weapon from his waistband and jabs the HK tightly into his forehead. Rafael pulls back, the look of the gun persuades him to plead his case.

"One of these days, a light is going to go on in your thick head. Now, tell me what you've been up to?"

Rafael is sweating, not sure if Jeff is going to use the gun this time. "Nothing, I swear. Just laying low until I can collect. I haven't spoken to anyone."

"So how did you know he was dead?"

Rafael exhales but only for a moment. "There's a brain in here somewhere, cabron."

Jeff continues. "You told me you wouldn't leave the house until we had the money."

"I got nervous, I didn't feel safe."

"There were five of us when this all started, now there are two. I know it wasn't me." Jeff holds the HK steady as if he has made up his mind. "Then who the fuck is it?"

Rafael moves his hand. "I don't have any weapon, I'm just reaching for something, okay?"

Jeff nods as Rafael's hand reaches into his back pocket.

Jeff is astonished as Rafael holds up a digital Panasonic recorder.

"Okay, I admit it," says Rafael. "I took it. A little insurance, you might say."

Jeff still has the gun firmly angled at his forehead. "So, it was you."

"Yes and it might tell us who will be responsible for our deaths before the week is out. Interested now?"

0935 HOURS (ART)

In a Buenos Aires police cell Sallum sits quietly in the corner, his hands cuffed to a steel rod cemented into the floor.

The police commissar enters the room and sits across from Sallum. He opens a file and lays it in front of him. He lights a cigarette but doesn't offer one to the prisoner.

"What brings you to Buenos Aires?"

Sallum's eyes are fixed on the ground. "Business."

The commissar ticks off a line in his notebook. "What business?"

Sallum's eyes return to the present. "I've been through all that with your colleagues."

The commissar puts out the cigarette in the well used ashtray. "Well, I like the sound of your voice. So tell me."

"Import export. You can look at the papers for yourself. The Saudi Embassy will be glad to help."

The commissar takes out a brown envelope and empties out the contents. Out come a successive file of black and white portraits—grainy images of the wanted gang.

"Look at the faces please."

Sallum glances downward, realizing he will not be caught with his guard down. He attempts to retain an air of authority and shakes his head slowly. The Commissar pushes another photo onto the desk.

"How about him?"

Sallum tries not to pause, to appear convincing. "No."

The Commissar looks carefully, tries to detect any sign of weakness.

"I don't think you even looked."

Sallum peers for a second time. "I'm sorry, I would like to help but I've never seen any of these men."

The Commissar nods.

Sallum returns a look of defiance, a look that says: 'I am not from your world, you know nothing about me'.

The phone rings and the Commissar picks it up. He mumbles into the receiver and then stares at Sallum.

He thinks for a moment and then stands. "We have nothing on him."

The policeman can't believe what he is hearing. "Pero, Señor?"

The commissar has already lit another cigarette. "While we still have some semblance of democracy in this country, we cannot keep him. Let him go. That's an order."

1135 HOURS (ART)

At the safe house, Rafael pours another beer. There are some glasses and a few empty Quilmes cans on the table.

"She left it on the table. What was I supposed to do? You never know when these things might come in useful."

Jeff holds the Panasonic recorder in his hand. "I'm surprised. Kind of unprofessional of her."

"Exactly, like she wasn't bothered if one of us helped ourselves. You don't speak Arabic, do you?"

Jeff shakes his head and takes a gulp of beer.

"Thought not. She probably knew that when she played it, none of us would understand. So, I had it translated. Interested?"

Rafael opens up his laptop and opens the MP3 file. He presses the play button. A voice starts up, American but with a slight Arab accent, the kind of voice you might hear selling t-shirts on Canal Street in New York:

"I'd like to order two tickets to Dubai. Business class, leaving early on the tenth and returning the evening of the twentieth. I'll need a rental car when I arrive."

Rafael clicks the computer and the audio stops.

"It's just a guy booking tickets to the Emirates at JFK." Jeff reaches for the handgun, pulls down on the safety. "Doesn't sound like him."

"You fool. It's her. Don't you see? Think about it. She's been playing us all along." His voice sounds nervous, unsure.

Jeff levels the gun at Rafael's temple.

1932 HOURS (ART)

At the Tortoni Cafe, the Emir sits towards the rear. He is a commanding man with a natural sense of authority. His voice is deep and balanced, each vowel perfectly pronounced. "Do you think they know?"

It is just before dark, the only witnesses to the meeting are a few passers-by heading home. Nobody is likely to overhear them.

"I saw their eyes when they looked at the photos, the corpses. Something isn't right." Sallum looks up at the frown on the Emir's face. "What's that? How can they know? And if they do, why would they let me go?"

The Emir responds quickly to dispel any concerns in his operative. "They know nothing. They are just fishing for Arabs, offering up photos, shaking something loose."

But Sallum has more questions. "We have the names? Only a few days since the robbery?"

The Emir smiles at this. "I told you, we have our source."

"This source might work both ways; for them as well as us."

"I assure you that is not the case."

Sallum takes a sip of his coffee. A crease appears across his brow, he will not back off. "I need to know."

"Know what?"

"What you know."

The Emir thinks for a moment. "Okay, it works like this. The CIA think they've turned a source so he informs and pockets a few thousand a week for the trouble. However, we know he's an informer and we pay him even better. We use him to feed false information. Let them spend their time arresting brothers in New York City for all we care!"

Sallum is relieved to hear the confidence in his voice. "Serves them right, they shouldn't serve the devil."

"Exactly."

A taxi screeches to a halt on Avenida Dorrego. The car sits at the intersection and the engine idles. Jeff follows Rafael as he crosses the road. He turns on his headset.

Rafael stops in the middle of the road, stares down the taxi driver. He moves his hand to the small of his back.

Jeff presses the button and whispers. "Rafael?"

Rafael continues to fixate on the driver.

Jeff presses the button and speaks a little louder this time. "Rafael. Stand down!"

Rafael finally talks. "Jeff, there's something different here."

Jeff answers immediately. "No, he's just a regular Radio Taxi."

But Rafael is fixated with the taxi driver. "It's his eyes, Jeff. I've seen him before."

Rafael pulls his gun out and points it directly at the windshield.

"You're seeing things. Stand down, now! That's an order!"

Jeff pulls off his intercom and runs towards Rafael. But he is too late.

Rafael shoots two slugs into the front tire which promptly explodes.

The taxi driver stares at Rafael for a brief second, recognizing the look of insanity. He opens the door and runs off down the avenue.

"What the fuck, Rafael!" shouts Jeff.

Rafael moves inside the car and begins to check the taxi cab. He opens up the glove compartment, rips out the back foam trying to find something. Anything.

Jeff pounces on his back and drags him from the car. He pulls his right arm behind his back and disarms him, opening the magazine and letting it drop to the street.

2053 HOURS (ART)

They arrive back at the Palermo safe house and Jeff leaves Rafael alone with his thoughts.

Rafael pours himself a beer as Jeff unloads the magazine and lays the gun on the table. He asks him in a quiet voice. "Want to explain what that was all about?"

Rafael takes out each 9mm bullet and reinserts them into the magazine. "I just thought it was him." His voice is dejected, defeated.

Jeff sits down next to him. "Look, Rafael, this isn't Fallujah. What's gotten into you?"

Rafael holds his head in his hands.

Jeff continues. "He was just a regular Porteño, for god's sake—a Taxista trying to make a peso or two in this shit hole!"

"Those dark eyes, fuck they all look alike. I'm sorry Jeff. I didn't mean to cause any more trouble"

Jeff pats him on the shoulder. "Look, maybe you should be reading something other than the Crusades."

A solitary light bulb hangs from the ceiling. Jeff closes the book and places it back on the shelf.

The phone rings and they both look at each other. Jeff takes the gun, takes out the magazine and places it in the safe.

He picks up the phone.

"Hola."

It's Susan. "Thank God, you're okay. I was starting to get worried."

He can almost believe her for a second. "You heard?"

"He seemed like a loose end. It might not be the worst thing for all of you."

Jeff looks at Rafael. "He was a friend."

"He knew the risks, I'm sorry."

"Do you have anything on the killer?"

"He's professional and not making any mistakes."

"That much we know."

"Anything I can do, just let me know."

"Don't worry, Susan. We can look after ourselves."

He cuts the phone and turns to Rafael as a look of understanding runs between them. "Now she knows," says Jeff.

"It's our best shot, believe me."

"We'll see about that."

Rafael turns to leave, then stops. "Remember Sergeant Gunny?"

"Yeah, at the sniper school."

"Right. Well, when I signed up he took me under his wing, showed me the ropes. He drummed it into me: let the enemy come to you. Go to them and you make yourself vulnerable. Let the fight come to you. It never fails."

Jeff nods in agreement. "That's if we get a chance to fight."

JANUARY 18, 0841 HOURS (ART)

A pair of Porteños walk towards the Tortoni Cafe.

Emir watches them closely from a concealed booth at the rear, until they are safely out of earshot. He reaches over the table and passes over a small brown briefcase. Sallum runs his hands over the briefcase, admires the dark brown leather, the fine stitching.

Sallum fixes his eyes in a stare as Emir explains what is before him.

"It's not much alone but then, with this and God's will, the blast will create a contaminated area the size of..."

He hands him the small phial enveloped by a sponge-lined box.

Sallum finishes the sentence: "...a city?"

"Exactly. We will strike with maximum potency, spread terror and confusion."

Sallum places the case beneath the table. "When do I leave?"

"Have patience, my child. The moment is close. Our brothers will prepare your path."

"I am honored to be chosen."

"As long as the thieves are still out there, our honor demands they must die."

He places the photos of the remaining known team members on the table: Jeff and Rafael. Sallum takes the photo, runs his hands over them and places them in his top pocket.

"In'sh Allah."

Sallum turns to leave but the Emir touches his hand gently, pulls him closer. "In the book of sura it is written: Mohammed is God's apostle. Those who follow must be ruthless to the infidel."

He lets go of Sallum and finishes his coffee. He watches him confidently glide through the front door out onto the Calle Florida.

He melts into the morning crowd.

2227 HOURS (ART)

There is no light in the safe house apart from the beam of an LED flashlight to lead the way along the corridor.

Rafael pulls a large object along the length of the corridor. "Where do you want it, I mean, him?"

Jeff calls down from the second floor. "Bring him upstairs."

Rafael grabs the body by the head and a lump of hair comes off in his hand.

"Ah, boludos!" He throws the wad onto the carpet.

"For Christ's sake, be careful with him," Jeff says.

Instead, Jeff comes down the stairs and helps lift the corpse by the shoulders, Rafael takes the legs and they head upstairs.

Rafael drops the body in a chair, buttons up the shirt, cleans it up. He stares into the opaque eyes, tries to tape them open.

Jeff brushes what is left of his hair. He gives up and places a cap on his head. "Even when he was alive, he looked half dead."

"Put a little color in his cheeks, some lipstick, you'd be amazed."

Jeff watches Rafael apply the makeup. From afar this should appear lifelike, at least for the purpose that they intended.

"When you're about to drop someone, you don't spend a lot of time checking their skin tone."

Rafael applies the last makeup. He stands back to check his work.

"Looks good to me."

Jeff cleans up the mess and throws the residue in the garbage. "Okay, that's it. Now we wait."

JANUARY 19, 0615 HOURS (ART)

The sun appears early and shines a dark yellow hue against the rear garden wall. They can already hear the screeches and calls of the various wild macaws that live in the overhanging jacaranda trees.

Rafael has made coffee and passes a mug over to Jeff. "Does this guy have a motive, or is it purely religious?"

Jeff piles in the sugar and swirls the spoon around a few times. "He had a family, once. A wife, a young child, an elderly father who worked the fields."

"So what went wrong?"

"They disappeared."

"How?"

He takes a long swig from the coffee mug.

"He left for work one morning and looked back to see a missile flying towards his house."

"Don't tell me, one of ours."

"He returned to a pile of rubble and what was left of his family."

"Jesus."

"The grief turned him into Allah's most fearsome warrior."

1139 HOURS (ART)

Outside of the metropolis of Buenos Aires the wind drifts constantly through the tall pampas grass. In the hazy distance a few cattle graze. In this vastness the cows look like ships afloat on a immense, tempestuous sea.

A cell phone rings, breaking the silence.

Susan walks over the grass towards the remnants of an old estancia.

"Yes."

She continues walking, her head nodding in agreement.

"Of course. But we have to be certain...I'm sorry, I must know it was them!" She pauses. "What about the Arab—has he been found yet? Without him the whole network falls apart. We'll be able to bag a few more in the process."

She walks on across the grass and steps onto the house terrace.

"Oh, let's just say I'm collecting a few extra funds." She laughs coyly into the phone. "Well, yes, of course. Perhaps a few new items. When a girl cracks the Al

Qaeda cell in South America and prevents a major terrorist attack up north, I think she's earned her keep,
don't you?"

A smile plays on her lips as she snaps the cell
phone closed. She heads toward a small thicket of trees,
the only trees in this flat sea of tall grass. She takes out
a map, checks the bearings again.

The cell phone rings again. She waits a few seconds then answers. "Yes?"

"Don't move."

Susan scours the horizon but sees no sign of movement. "Jeff?"

"Stay perfectly still."

Susan looks outwardly nervous, though she tries
hard to make her voice sound calm. "There's something
wrong, Jeff. I can hear it in your voice." She looks down
at her feet.

"Looks like you've discovered it."

"Jeff, I don't like the sound of your voice."

Jeff is unmoved by her tone. "Five pounds of plastic explosive. Move and they'll be scraping bits off the
taxi cabs in Buenos Aires."

Susan freezes, stares ahead, every nerve in her
body switches off. He can see her mouth gasp, she does-
n't want to believe. The movement is involuntary and
she soon regains her poise.

"Jeff, why?" Susan is still frozen. "Why would you
do this?"

From up in the trees a slight rustle and a few leaves
fall. Jeff swings down from the tree, hits the ground
gracefully, rubs his hands to get the feeling back.

115

A few seconds pass before Rafael joins him at his side. Jeff walks toward her slowly.

He stops a few paces short. "You let us down."

"It's not so simple." The tone of her voice shows she has regained some of her poise.

She moves slightly.

"I wouldn't do that if I were you."

"What the hell am I standing on?"

Rafael steps forward. "Iranian C4 rigged up to a simple trigger. An old cell phone with a pre-programmed number. Shape charge. It'll take you, not us."

Susan turns from Rafael and faces Jeff. "Jeff, turn it off. Now!"

Jeff looks over at Rafael who shrugs his shoulders, as if ready to detonate.

Rafael holds up a small cell phone.

Susan tries another route. "What happened to Sallum?"

"You know what happened."

"I don't. That's why I'm here. I know nothing about him."

Jeff barely hears her voice and continues. "He made his attack on the safe house, just like we knew he would... You told him where we were, you told him everything..."

FLASHBACK

The sky is dark, a quarter moon shines in through the skylight. Somewhere in the distance wails the siren of a police car as it speeds down to the Capital Federal.

116

Sallum lies silently, invisible against the grey sky, no movement. He is alone with his thoughts.

The window looks out onto the quiet street below and across to the house directly opposite. Barely an inch of black metal emerges from a circular hole cut into the glass.

Sallum holds the gun steady. With deep breaths he controls the rhythm of his breathing.

From below, he detects a slight movement. It is all that it takes to alert his senses—a minute movement across the first floor window. A man, definitely. Carefully, Sallum presses his eyes firmly against the scope.

There is no mistaking a human face. A flash of hair and then beneath it the skin of a man's forehead. Yes, he knows he has it, target acquired.

He steadies the rifle, checks his breath, lines the sight with the man's head.

Gently, he pulls the trigger.

All that he hears is the curtailed slash of broken glass. Then 'chink', the sound of a bullet making contact.

Through the high powered scope, the bullet slams into the man's head. The body doubles over, fragments of skull splinter against the far wall. Sallum pauses for any movement. He waits patiently, but finds nothing.

He breathes slowly, releasing the tension between his shoulders.

His job is done. After a few seconds he begins to break down the rifle and exits the building.

Susan looks up helplessly. She is pleading now.

Jeff tries not to look her in the eyes as he starts to speak. "He was a good soldier, he did what any of us would have done. He followed his orders."

Rafael walks up to her side. "And he paid the ultimate price."

Susan looks over at Jeff. "But there were bodies found at the scene?"

Jeff retains an air of superiority. "Yes, we thought you'd ask that one."

Susan is losing patience with the game they are playing. "Oh, Jeff just tell me, will you?"

"One was Sallum, the other was Sergio."

"Sergio." She is still trying to put all the pieces together, figure out what happened in the safe house.

"Yes, you see he was dead anyway. We figured he wouldn't mind us imposing on him for a good cause."

Susan almost collapses as she understands what went wrong. "I see," she says almost bewilderedly.

Jeff continues. "At some stage the federal police will figure it out. But we'll be long gone, right?"

Jeff notices the diamond hanging from her neck, the same rock he gave her a week ago.

Susan gives out a helpless sigh. "So. What do you want now?"

Jeff takes a few seconds. He is beginning to enjoy being on the controlling end. "They died because of you, Susan. We just want to know why."

Rafael holds up the Nokia cell phone to make his point. "And the truth this time."

She looks at both of them, scrutinizing their expressions. "Guys, you knew what this mission was all about."

"I want to hear it from your lips," Jeff says.

Susan smiles. "Not here. Surely we can find someplace more comfortable."

Rafael springs forward. "You'll stay where you are, bitch! Inches from death, just like we've been for the past few weeks."

She looks towards them, angry now. Her lips clenched in a tight grin, her fist held tightly at her side. "You fucking bunch of cowards! All of you. You don't mind taking the money until there's a risk." She stares over at Jeff who merely looks away. "Every risk has a price, it's basic economics."

"Just tell us the truth, Susan. We're done with your dramatics."

Susan sighs deeply. "Okay, you want the truth. The Ambassador's death was a blow to our prestige, a major setback. Worse, he knew Al Qaeda was gearing up for a big hit. All the old tricks we'd used in the past hadn't worked. That's when the big shots higher up came up with a plan."

She hesitates, looks down at the ground as if checking for the exact spot. "A big robbery, an Argentine job, if you like. With al Qaeda, honor is absolute, revenge must be taken so they send their best man. We leak the culprits and watch them, eventually we find the assassin. Keep tabs on him and he'll lead us to the cell."

Rafael pulls out the Nokia again. "Sure, a classic plan. But you lied to us."

"Christ, am I dealing with a bunch of kids here?" she snorts. "This is war, damn it! Deceit is the most important weapon in any arsenal."

Jeff stands before Rafael and places his palm on the cell phone. "What if she's right? I mean who's fooling whom? We all need the money."

Rafael cannot believe what he is hearing. "That bitch told Al-Qaeda where we were. I don't think that was part of the bargain!" He looks towards Jeff, who is clearly having doubts and Rafael can see it. "Come on, Jeff. Are we going to do this, or not?"

Jeff looks into Susan's eyes, sees a glimmer of fear. Her tone is changing, each vowel turns brighter. She appeals to him again:

"Okay, three of your men died. But if the attack had occurred, thousands would have been killed, not to mention the economy. America can't take it again. You guys are all heroes."

Jeff turns towards Rafael. "Okay, we take the money and walk. Right now we're free and rich. If we press the button we're fugitives the rest of our lives."

He glances over at Rafael but sees only an intense anger in his eyes, as if a fuse has been lit inside.

"Who the fuck are you to make the choice?"

"I'm your commanding officer. There's been enough killing already."

Jeff sees a slight smile spread across Susan's teeth. Happy, not at the fact that she might be saved, but that she might have won the argument. But Rafael is having nothing of it.

"What about Sergio and his wife?" He looks back at Susan with a sneer. "Their boy, too. You sent them to their death. How can you justify that?"

Susan shrugs this away as if she is losing interest.

"She's right, Rafi. It's time to walk."

Rafael looks back to Jeff, can't believe what he says.

Susan is losing her patience. "Come on, you idiots!"

Her voice is ragged, she is at her wit's end. Rafael stands motionless. He holds the cell phone in front of him and presses the power button.

Susan knows the tide has turned in her favor. "You have both made a lot of mistakes but the most dangerous was to underestimate me."

The wind picks up speed across the Pampas and the trees rustle.

Jeff snaps his head to see somebody standing barely six feet behind, a pistol in his outstretched hand, the barrel pointing directly at the back of his head.

He recognizes the officer from earlier in the Faena Hotel.

"Slowly. Hand it over."

Jeff can see the anger in Rafael's eyes, as if a flame within has been ignited. For a moment he thinks he might veer towards the insane; blow them all away. Rafael's hand drops away, clear for all to see.

The officer closes in. "Give me the phone, or you both die!"

Susan is still stuck in place. "Do as he says. Give it to him."

The tone of her voice tells the tale, they threatened to kill her and by so doing have signed their death warrant.

"They'll kill us anyway. Hell, if we're going to die, we'll take you bastards with us!" Jeff is surprised at how calm he sounds as he looks over at Rafael.

Susan raises her hands. Her eyes too are concentrated on Rafael. "Jeff, tell him to put that stupid thing down. Take the money and get on with your life."

Jeff turns away from her.

"Don't listen to her!"

Rafael looks at Jeff and then back to Susan. He hesitates.

Jeff sees her face flinch as the phone falls into the mud. She steps quickly away from where the bomb is buried. Behind him he can see that the army officer holds the gun level with Rafael's head.

Susan walks calmly past him. "Do it!"

A shot rings out. The noise of the bullet rustles pigeons from the tree tops.

Jeff throws himself into the mud, shields his face with his hands, but the bullet is not for him. He looks up. Six feet to his right lies Rafael, face down in the mud, body crumpled in agony, blood pouring from the side of his head.

Jeff reaches out to grab the phone, which is barely four feet away. He scrambles through the dirt, on hands and knees.

But his hand is six inches short as a sharp jab crunches him in the ribs. Susan stands above him, stamps hard against his hand and twists her heel against his palm.

"Now, what was it you were saying?"

The officer has appeared, a Walther 9mm pointed at Jeff. The officer stands back, his pistol still aimed at Jeff's head.

"Where is the money?" says Susan.

Jeff recognizes the look on her face; a mixture of desire, passion and, above all, contempt. "Fuck off, bitch."

"Tell me where the money is or we kill you right here." She stares at him, a cold, steely gaze. She is all business now.

Jeff laughs as he spits out blood from his mouth. "You'll kill me anyway, whatever I say."

She twists the heel of her shoe into his palm. The pain is intense but he knows it will be over soon. He attempts a smile which comes out more like a grimace.

"You never give up, do you?"

She's not giving up and stamps her foot again.

Jeff tries to scream but it comes out more as a whimper. "Go fuck yourself!"

The officer walks over and faces Susan. "This is pointless, we'll never break him."

1547 HOURS (ART)

In a dry river bed, Jeff can hear the steady sound of steel hitting the dry, dusty soil. Slowly he realizes it is the soldiers busy digging holes at the base of one of the few trees to dot the landscape.

123

Jeff pulls his legs up to his chin and rests his head for a moment. He's obviously in great pain.

He looks over at Rafael's body as the blood seeps from the wound on his head. Mixed with rain, it forms a pool beneath the listless body.

Then he looks over at Susan. She has found something, something that doesn't belong. She starts scratching away at the leaves and then digging with her own shovel. The sound changes as she hits something underneath; loose soil, freshly dug.

"It's here, I've found it!"

The officer looks up as a shot rings out from further down the valley.

Right next to him, the soldier's eyes bulge from his skull, his knees bend over as he slumps to the ground. Falling forward, his body crashes into Jeff's chest. He is stunned by the weight of the body, the blood jetting from the hole in the back of the head.

The officer takes cover behind a tree, as Susan drops the two yellow canvas bags and runs towards him.

"What was that?

The officer is shaken. He had thought they were alone. "How should I know?"

Susan looks over at Jeff. "Just finish him off! Can't you fucking get that right?"

Jeff looks into the gun aimed at him. He holds the soldier's dead body in front of him as a shield, hopes for the best.

Two more shots ring out.

Jeff feels the impacts hit the motionless body on top of him. A splatter of blood flies across his face as he reaches out and grabs the mud-soaked pistol. Behind the dead body, he is relatively secure. He slides back the muzzle, checks the magazine: four rounds. He clicks it back in the handle. Loaded.

With the dead body held in front of him, Jeff edges back towards the ridge, inches at a time using his legs, dragging the corpse along the way. Another bullet slams into the corpse, Jeff tries to shrink himself into the mud. He can barely see Susan and the officer leaning out from the tree, firing at will, point blank. There is no way to get the pistol free, get a clear shot without exposing himself.

Two more shots, but this time further away, behind the ridge that gives him an inch of cover. Then another shot and a bullet ricochets and hits the mud a couple of feet away. They are getting closer, he has to run for it.

"Ha!"

Jeff stands up, all six foot of him, arms tight around the corpse.

Phud! Phud! The bullets keep on coming. He stumbles backward, struggles to keep hold of the corpse, gunfire all around. Jeff waits until he is five yards from the ridge and then he drops the corpse.

He runs the last few yards as bullets pound around him into the ridge. One last gasp and he hurls himself over the top. With a crash he falls into a pile of leaves. Stunned, he stares up to the sky as somebody peers above him.

This time the unlikely face of Tulio. "She said you run like a girl. I reckon she was right all along!"

125

Tulio wears a black leather jacket turned up against the rain, holds a Czech VZ-52 rifle above the ridge. Next to him, Isabella smiles briefly. He is a little shocked to see her holding an M-16 carbine. She wears blue leather boots and a matching quilted polo jacket, the rain has washed her hair over her face.

Jeff can't help but smile.

Jeff turns back to Tulio. "I thought you were dead."

Tulio holds the gun steady, looks through the scope. "Out of action for a while, amigo, that's all."

Jeff points over the ridge. "The money's down there."

Tulio nudges Jeff in the ribs and he flinches. "Isa knew you'd stash it here. Guess it holds some kind of importance for you two."

Jeff looks over at Isabella. He smiles, knowing that she has come for him. He points to her rifle. "Know how to use that thing?"

Isabella turns back to the battle. "Saved your life, didn't I?"

Jeff checks chamber in his pistol and peers over the ridge. "You guys are going to give me plenty of cover. Just keep them pinned down. Tulio, you take Susan, I'll deal with this one. Ready?"

Isabella smiles at him and takes position at the ridge line. She holds the rifle tight at her shoulder, and slots in a new magazine. She looks down the scope and points the rifle towards Susan, She fires a short burst, then turns the gun to the left and fires another burst.

Jeff tightens his grip on the Walther. There are only four rounds left, he will have to make them count. He runs, keeping his head down, making a small target. He hides behind a large boulder and feels the earth explode around him. More gunfire, this time from Susan.

The officer suddenly appears closer. He fires, runs and ducks. He makes for a difficult target, switching from tree to tree.

Jeff pulls back and manages several covering shots. Around him, the tree bark pings, a wooden splinter hits him in the face, just below the eye. The pain stuns him, blurs his vision. More gunfire echoes through the valley and then only silence. He lifts his head, hears the guns reloading.

He has two shots left, this is the time to pounce.

Jeff jumps out from the tree, exposed. He holds the gun out in front, lines the sight to his eye. The officer looks up at him, a frown suddenly shrouds his face as he clicks the magazine into place, cocks the gun. But all he hears is a click, a suicide click as the gun jams.

Jeff pulls the trigger.

1603 HOURS (ART)

An eerie silence covers the entire valley.

Susan is now surrounded. Her gun sits between her forearm and her shoulder, desperate, her finger still on the trigger.

Tulio stands over her. She clutches her shoulder, blood drips down her arm. He holds the VZ 52 steady against her body.

Jeff takes the officer's pistol, pulls out the jammed cartridge and looks over at Isabella.

She returns a look of defiance. "I forgot to mention, my father fought in the Malvinas."

1635 HOURS (ART)

Jeff throws the two yellow bags before Susan. He holds up the trigger in front of her.

"Now, where were we?"

Fear begins to spread across her face as she looks over at Isabella. "He's lied to you. You don't know what he's been up to all this time."

Isabella shrugs and holds up the gun. "I'm the one holding the gun. That doesn't make me so foolish."

Susan laughs out loud. "You'd really risk your life to save this pathetic loser?"

Susan turns back to Jeff. "Well, let me fill you in, sister. For the past few weeks he's been screwing me every chance he gets."

She parts her blouse to show the diamond that hangs on a gold chain. "That's right, where do you think I got this?"

The wind lashes on Jeff's face as he tightens his grip on the pistol. "Don't listen to her."

Isabella looks into Jeff's eyes. "Is it true?"

The tip of her rifle turns slowly away from Susan. Her finger still on the trigger, he notices her hand starting to tremble with anxiety.

"Isa, I got involved so I could pay my debts and we could be together. You know that."

Susan laughs out loud. "Oh you sad fool! Sitting at home grieving over this loser, meanwhile he's screwing every mina in sight!"

Susan sneers. "Kill me out of jealousy or just kill me for revenge but you should know the truth. Girl to girl." Susan stares at Isabella, her eyes full of sympathy.

But Isabella doesn't see her, she is still looking at Jeff. "Jeff?"

He starts to say something to her: "The truth is..."

Tulio steps forward. "Everything she says is lies. Complete lies, Isabella," he says.

Isabella looks over at Tulio.

Tulio continues. "We all decided to give her a diamond. I tell you, it was professional, nothing happened between them."

Slowly Isabella's frown disappears and she lowers the gun. Jeff looks over at Tulio for a reaction but there is none.

Susan pulls up a gun, points it at Jeff and fires.

The bullet hits Jeff in his side and he falls down clutching the wound. Tulio kicks the gun away from Susan but the damage has been done. She sneers triumphantly.

"I told you not to push me. You bastard, I told you..."

Isabella raises the M-16.

JANUARY 20, 0624 HOURS (ART)

Jeff lies motionless in a hospital, hooked up to several machines. He is conscious but stuck somewhere between the here and now. His mind drifts somewhere over the Pampas, above the wisps of grass and the distant grazing cattle.

Jeff's voice: "Emptiness, a familiar emotion. Every kill is your own, nobody can share it. At the end we are all alone with our thoughts. Nobody can help you through it. Nobody."

Suddenly he is brought back to the presence by a sound, a loud sound.

Tulio knocks on the door but receives no reply. He enters and sees Jeff is patched up on the side of his torso, his chest rising with the oxygen tube taped to his mouth. Jeff moves his head and sees a blurred image of Tulio.

"You're okay, Jeff. I'll just talk, go ahead and nod if you can hear me."

Jeff's head moves slowly.

"Okay, well you might have a few questions. My disappearance seems to have caused some friction in the team."

Again Jeff moves his head slowly.

"What was that?" says Tulio.

"Just a bit."

"You see, the easy point was disappearing."

"Why is that?"

"It was obvious they were on to us. The only way I'd survive was if they thought I was dead."

Jeff pulls out the oxygen tube. He tries to say some more but his mouth is too dry. He points to a glass of water that sits on his bed side tray. Tulio passes it over and he takes a big sip.

"How?"

"I knew Sallum was on my tail, he was working his way down the list. So I gave him the switch. He followed me to a gay club in Belgrano. You know, one of those bath house places you warned me against when we started this job. I saw someone, my height and build, went upstairs and made sure that Sallum followed. Then I slipped out. I told the stranger there was a cute guy waiting for him, a real stud. Off he went, into the darkness. In that situation he never noticed anything. Let alone that it wasn't me."

Jeff is suddenly awake. He leans over to Tulio. "He had your license, your credit cards. He sent them with a severed hand, tied to a brick and threw them through the window."

"Yes, I bet that got Rafael's attention. See, that was the easy part. As the stranger went off for his date, I picked his pocket. Exchanged all his cards for mine, left the wallet on the bar."

Jeff drinks some more water. "Poor bastard, never knew what hit him."

"I figured I was no use to anyone, I had done my job. I hope you never thought I'd abandoned you."

Jeff tries to get up but thinks better of it. "Abandoned? I thought you were dead."

"That was the downside to my plan. I phoned Isabella a couple of days back to find out what was up. She hadn't heard from you. So, I came here to collect my cut."

Jeff looks toward Isabella. She slips her hand into his. He looks up at her, he has so many questions, she can read it in his eyes.

131

"I don't want to talk about it," she replies.

Jeff suddenly sighs, all the pressure is starting to vanish before him. "I've made so many mistakes."

She looks into his eyes and smiles. "We've all made mistakes, Jeff. I just want things back the way they were."

Tulio can't stand mawkish sentimentality. "Look I'm here for the money, not another Argentine family wedding with all the fittings. I might give that a miss."

"You're not missing my wedding," she says half seriously.

Jeff sits up, the strength starting to flow through his body. "At least we can afford one now."

Isabella looks away nervously.

"There's one last thing.," Jeff says. Jeff pulls himself up and swings his legs over the side of the bed. "The money, I know. Someone was bound to get to it at some stage. I've been lying here all night thinking about it."

Tulio starts to look a little worried. "I hope you have good news."

Jeff reaches beneath the bed and pulls out three bags. One for each of them.

0728 HOURS (ART)

Jeff sits in bed, reading an old 'Hola' magazine.

Jeff's voice reverberates around his head: "I was anxious to get on with my new life, maybe take Isabella for a vacation along the way. The doctors had warned me my wounds would take a few weeks to heal. I would need to change the bandages several times a day to avoid infection where the bullet had done its damage. But I'd survive this just as I had always before. Sure it would leave a scar but my mind was set. I was going to leave this life forever, even if it was the last thing I ever did."

A brief knock on the door stirs him from his thoughts.

Colonel Ambrose, accompanied by two armed police officers, enters the room.

Ambrose stares at the patient and then down at the yellow duffel bag. He kneels down and goes to work on it, scooping up the money in his fat hands. Then he starts counting, realizes it will take forever before zipping it shut and turning it over to the officers.

"You two, stand down. I'll take it from here. Wait outside in the hall. It will make things a lot easier to explain."

They exit the room.

Jeff offers his hand. "I've been expecting you."

Ambrose seems angered by Jeff's calmness. "All I want to know is why you murdered two of my Argentine officers and a CIA agent?"

"Ah, that."

"Yes, that little item."

"Because they tried to kill us."

"You were supposed to be working together."

"It was self defense."

Ambrose paces back and forth. "Yeah, right. I might want to believe you, Tully, but try explaining that to the Agency. We have your fingerprints all over the murder scene..."

Jeff is still calm. "You might have my prints but what you don't have is the truth."

Ambrose sneers at him. "Truth? How about the facts."

"Susan was playing you. She lied to us all."

Ambrose stops pacing. "Why should I believe you?"

Jeff reaches into his bedside table. He opens a drawer. "Because her band of thieves planned to kill us all and snatch the money for themselves."

He throws an envelope onto the bed and Ambrose peeks inside.

Jeff continues while he has the upper hand. "Three first class tickets to JFK, made out in their names. With that kind of money she could have been anywhere in the world within twenty-four hours."

Ambrose looks at the tickets, the cogs of his mind turning over. He is stunned as he turns to Jeff. "You can't expect me to hand the money over. I mean, there will be an official inquiry..."

Jeff continues. "We did the job, we've kept our part of the bargain."

Ambrose shakes his head slowly. "As I said, that's not possible now."

Jeff suddenly becomes calm again. "I'm afraid that is where you are wrong."

Ambrose laughs arrogantly at first, but the laughter dies as he realizes that Jeff is completely serious.

"Susan had mentioned an al Qaeda hit somewhere in the north," Jeff states.

"That's right. We feared the attack would go down, that's why we—"

"What if I have it?"

Ambrose turns, looks down worried. "It?"

"The weapon."

There is an evocative silence as Jeff takes a sip of water.

"That might change the matter considerably." Ambrose puts the envelope away and looks up, perplexed. "What exactly are we talking about?"

"To be honest, I'm not exactly sure."

Ambrose retains an air of superiority. "Where is it?"

"Like I told you, it's in a safe place. Now, we need to talk."

0957 HOURS (ART)

At the Abasto Shopping Center the regular calm sounds of families having fun are swapped for screams as there is a mass exodus.

A swat team pours into the food court. Mothers and fathers sense the danger and panic sets in. They head for the rotating doors that lead out onto Avenida Cordoba.

The swat team races up the escalators and take up positions next to the McDonald's restaurant, whose presence is underlined by a large Kosher sign. To the side is a bank of lockers. Ambassador Ambrose moves forward, produces a key and carefully opens locker number nine.

Inside lies a briefcase, nothing else.

Ambrose approaches carefully. He reaches for it and lays it on the marble floor. He flicks the hinge and unlocked, it flings upright and open.

Inside he finds a velvet pouch which he carefully opens to reveal a cushioned compartment. This he opens and looks at the contents: a phial of a dirty, brown liquid.

1446 HOURS (ART)

At the entrance to the Retiro train station, Tulio jumps out of the Ford Mustang and heads to the kiosk at the curb. He buys today's La Nacion paper and, reading a story just below the headline, walks back towards Jeff.

"So?"

"Nothing too incriminating." Tulio holds the newspaper open and begins to translate. "If CIA assassins were behind the killing of an Al Qaeda operative yesterday, it would be the latest chapter in a long history of U.S. covert action against terrorist foes best confronted with full force. As always, U.S. embassy officials declined any comment on the death of Rami Sallum Mohammad, nor would they confirm any covert activities in the Argentine capital."

Tulio dumps the newspaper in the nearest trash bin. Isabella is still in the driver's seat as she keeps the engine idling while Jeff pulls out the bags from the trunk.

Tulio walks over to Jeff and takes his bag. "Look after her. Apart from my father and what's in here, she's all I have."

Jeff looks into his eyes. He goes to shake his hand but hugs him instead. "I want to thank you."

Tulio knows there is more, something he is hiding deep inside. "What is it, Jeff?"

Jeff looks away, as a train exits the station, the horn echoing through the enormous building. "Nothing."

Tulio stoops to take the bag. Jeff grabs his arm. "You did a great job. It's just hard to believe it's over."

"I know."

Isabella joins in the goodbyes. She kisses her brother tenderly on the cheek.

Tulio heaves the heavy bag onto his back, waves one more time and joins the crowds that make their way across the platform to the awaiting train.

He doesn't look back, he just continues.

1505 HOURS (ART)

Isabella swerves onto Avenue Libertad. The car's top is down, the sun shines, it is a beautiful day. She revs the V8 engine and heads north away from the city.

It is hot, taxis move in and out of the hordes of tourists that for some reason or other, are attracted to this area. Not far away, legs, lots of legs walk along the sidewalks and bodies move to the sensual music of the Tango.

The scene is broken by a cartoñero.

He is followed by a three-legged dog who hobbles along beside him.

1512 HOURS (ART)

Jeff looks over at Isabella. Her eyes are on the road as he watches the breeze blow through her long, shiny hair.

Isabella turns towards Jeff whose eyes are still fixed on her.

"What are you thinking?"

He looks over as the Jorge Newberry airport recedes into the distance.

"Just how beautiful you look right now."

He smiles and turns to face forward though his thoughts are a million miles away.

Behind them the huge cranes of the dockyards recede into the distance. She makes a right and they exit the highway and head onto the open road, toward Los Olivos.

1513 HOURS (ART)

Up above, 18 floors to be precise, a man peers through a powerful Leica spotting scope. He watches the Ford Mustang as it drives away.

Emir Hassad stands up from the scope, pulls out a cell phone and pushes the call button.

FADE TO BLACK

www.AisleSeatBooks.com

Now that you've enjoyed this Movie Length Tale, you can help us turn it into a feature film.

On our web site you can give it an overall rating, you can rate it according to several specific factors, and you can even tell us who you would like to see cast in its principal roles. It's quick, fun, and easy.

Just log on to:

http://graybooks.net/aisleseatbooks/reader-feedback/reader-feedback-the-argentine-job

ABOUT THE AUTHOR

London born, a dual U.S./U.K. citizen, Michael Penhallow speaks four languages and has travelled widely through many distant corners of the world. It was a trip to the Tri Border Area, the lawless region that traverses the Argentina, Paraguay and Brazil borders, that inspired THE ARGENTINE JOB. A Nicholl Fellowship finalist, Oshun55 Award and American Screenplay winner, Michael is married and splits his time between San Francisco and New York.

Proof

Made in the USA
Charleston, SC
17 February 2012